To Ernie

with love & lots of
good wishes.

Celia Fremlin

KING OF THE WORLD

Further Titles by Celia Fremlin from Severn House

THE ECHOING STONES

KING OF
THE WORLD

Celia Fremlin

This first world edition published in Great Britain 1994 by
SEVERN HOUSE PUBLISHERS LTD of
9–15 High Street, Sutton, Surrey SM1 1DF.
First published in the USA 1994 by
SEVERN HOUSE PUBLISHERS INC., of
425 Park Avenue, New York, NY 10022.

British Library Cataloguing in Publication Data
Fremlin, Celia
    King of the World
    I. Title
    823.914 [F]

    ISBN 0-7278-4639-6 [cased]
    ISBN 0-7278-9015-8 [paper]

Typeset by Hewer Text Composition Services, Edinburgh.
Printed and bound in Great Britain by
Redwood Books, Trowbridge, Wiltshire.

Chapter 1

"Penny for the guy, Miss!" shrieked the importunate urchin, detaching himself from his companions and bouncing across Bridget's path. He shook at her a battered yoghourt pot, already rattling with coins. "Penny for the guy!"

He couldn't have been more than six years old, though his face, screwed up with aggressive purpose, looked almost adult under the harsh street lighting; a tiny cynical businessman, world-weary before his time.

Bridget shook her head. This was the third lot she'd encountered since getting off the bus, though it wasn't even November yet. Besides, her purse was deep in the bottom of her shoulder-bag, buried beneath her library book, her set of office keys, her translation notes, and a half-finished letter to her mother. The very thought of fishing for it with gloved hands was mildly exhausting.

And on top of all this, she would have to decide how much to give them. What did they actually have in mind when this obsolete word "penny" slid so effortlessly from their baby mouths? Even Bridget herself, at twenty-eight, could only just remember the upheaval and consternation when the old currency had disappeared for ever, and the familiar chant of "Twelve pence one shilling, twenty shillings one pound" was to be heard no more in the classrooms of the land. She remembered her father waxing indignant over the hidden price-rises involved. "Everything that cost a penny last week is now twopence-halfpenny!" he'd blustered; while her mother wrestled unhappily and in silence with the embarrassment of having to use the word "pee" when out shopping.

She walked briskly on through the damp evening, averting her face from the huddled little group who stood watching her with wary, judgmental eyes.

It was a rotten guy anyway, just a tattered oblong of school drawing-paper with a couple of round eyes scrawled on it in yellow crayon, amid a row of jagged teeth. No trouble had been taken over it at all. However poor you are, you could always take trouble, she reflected. Surely you could? Bridget herself had always taken trouble over everything. Not that she had ever been poor, but then poverty is only one of the obstacles that Life can put in a person's path. Such obstacles as Bridget had encountered she had overcome by her own efforts – or so she flattered herself.

"If it's worth doing at all it's worth doing properly" her father used to admonish her – quite unnecessarily, as it happened, for Bridget had been the sort of child who always did things properly. She never left her dolls' house without first tucking the plastic children up in their beds and propping the mother alongside the toy cooker in her blue-and-white check apron. Finally she would settle the black-trousered Daddy in his armchair (luckily his legs were flexible, he could both stand and sit) in front of the miniature television set, into which she would slot minuscule advertisements for soap-powder or ChocoFlakes, or something of the sort.

2

It was the same with school work. By the time she was in the Sixth Form she had built a reputation for being "brilliant" – "A high-flyer", which naturally she found very pleasing; though even at the time she had sometimes wondered whether she was *really* so brilliant? Or did she just work harder than anybody else?

Did it matter? Whatever it was, it had worked. It got her into Cambridge to read modern languages. It got her a first-class degree, followed by a well-paid job in an import export firm.

From then on, Bridget had gone from strength to strength, and had already achieved her original ambition. She was now a freelance interpreter and simultaneous translator, greatly in demand at international conferences both in Britain and abroad.

Reaching her own road, Bridget turned her thoughts to the evening ahead. Her flatmate would be in by now, and would already have taken from the Ansaphone the replies – if any – to their advertisement. In a way, Bridget hoped there wouldn't be any. It was true that the flat she and Diana were sharing was a good deal larger than they needed for just the two of them, even when you included the increasingly frequent and increasingly prolonged visits of Diana's boy-friend, Alistair. The flat had three good bedrooms as well as a large and elegantly proportioned sitting-room, with glass doors opening onto a south-facing balcony. The idea of taking in a third tenant was eminently sensible. There really was plenty of room, and the financial advantages of such an arrangement were too obvious to need much discussion.

But she and Diana were getting on so well as they were. Bridget had been afraid, when they first set up house together, that Diana's age – nearly ten years older than herself – would create some sort of a barrier to easy, day-to-day companionship. She had feared that the older woman might want to establish some sort of fixed routine for their life together; and this would not have suited Bridget's irregular life-style at all.

In the event, though, it was a non-problem. Diana also had a demanding job with irregular hours, and so they quickly fell into the habit of sharing meals only occasionally, when both happened to be at home, and of doing bits of housework whenever one or the other of them found the time. Thus an amiable, do-it-yourself regime was quickly established which suited them both. And as to Bridget's other fear – that the decade's difference in age might prove a barrier to companionship – this too proved unfounded. In fact, on the odd occasion – mostly late at night – when they were both at home and with time to chat, Bridget was constantly made aware that it was she, not Diana, who seemed to be taking the rôle of the wise older woman. Largely, she began to realise, this was thanks to Alistair; because, whatever the initial subject of their conversation, it always worked swiftly round to Diana's love-life. It was this that cancelled out – and indeed reversed – the age-gap; for it is a universal rule in these sort of heart-to-heart conversations that the one whose boy-friend it isn't inevitably finds herself in the rôle of comforter and counsellor to the one whose boy-friend it is.

By now, Bridget had arrived at Acorn House, the converted Victorian mansion in which she and Diana had made their home. As she mounted the wide front steps, slippery with fallen leaves, Bridget extracted her key, and found herself hoping quite desperately that Alistair wouldn't be there. A prospective tenant – or maybe several of them might have left messages on the Ansaphone. Appointments would then have to be made, maybe decisions reached this very evening, and she knew already exactly what Alistair's contribution to the decision-making would be. Spread-eagled against the sofa-back, his long legs stretched out to an amazing distance across the carpet, he would be relaxing, eyes closed, in an attitude of cosmic boredom, far above such mundane trivialities. Now and again he would half-open those heavy-lidded eyes and throw out such contributions as: "It'll be all the same in a hundred years" Or "You'll die if you worry, you'll die if you don't, so why-y-y worry!"

She prayed, so far as a godless person can pray, that he wouldn't be there.

Chapter 2

He was, though. Standing in the doorway of the sitting-room, still in her anorak and head-scarf, Bridget took in first those absurdly extended legs, ending in a pair of shapeless socks that someone must have knitted for him (not Diana, for God's sake?). Then, following the line from his shoeless feet upwards, she noted that his eyes were closed (as they usually were in company), and round his mouth hovered that utterly relaxed, utterly self-absorbed smile: the smile of a man enjoying some secret joke inside his head, a joke far too subtle and precious to be wasted on anyone of less rarefied sensibilities than his own.

"Hiya, beautiful!" he remarked, still not opening his eyes. "How's tricks? Howya doing?"

If she just crept away without answering, would he notice? Or would he go on murmuring Americanised platitudes into empty space while she disappeared into the kitchen and concocted something for her supper? It looked as if this was not, after all, to be an evening when she and Diana would be eating together. Bridget had no intention of preparing a meal for the three of them – why should she? Let Diana cope with him; he was hers, wasn't he?

Where *was* Diana anyway? They'd planned to spend

this evening together, going through the messages on the Ansaphone and deciding which applicants were worth following up. A third "Person" was what they'd specified in their advertisement, but that was only because they'd had a vague idea that "Third Woman" might lay them open to a charge of sexual discrimination, especially as the paper in which they'd inserted the advertisement was of a vaguely Left-wing slant. They'd agreed, though, between themselves, that only applications from females would be considered. Women were less trouble in every way: tidier, more anxious to conform, and a good deal less time-consuming. Though a very *young* man might be all right – a student, perhaps, spending his days on campus, and away for vacations. Someone not a day over twenty, anyway: the prospect of yet *another* large, ubiquitous, space-consuming middle-aged male about the place was daunting to both of them, though neither actually put this into words.

Above all, whoever came would have to be a *busy* person; out all day at some demanding job, and with lots of outside activities to fill her evenings. For any sort of shared life to be successful, from marriage downwards, the most important factor had nothing to do with shared interests, thought Bridget, nor even with shared values; it was a matter of being equally busy. If one member of the partnership had a great deal more leisure than the other, disaster loomed: the leisured one would feel neglected; the busy one, intolerably pressured.

Thinking about it now, Bridget reflected that it was this which had so far held her relatively aloof from the idea of marriage. Her job, which she loved, was a demanding one, and likely to become more so as success bred more success. Already she was feeling her

8

rare leisure hours to be precious beyond all calculation. Now and again, she'd tried to explain this to her mother, whose increasingly anxious hints about Bridget's still-single state were beginning to eat into their relatively pleasant relationship. "No, it's not that I hate men," Bridget had assured her mother. "Nothing like that at all. And I'd quite like to have children, later on. It's just . . ." and she remembered trying to choose the right words: "It's just – well – it's the unwritten part of the marriage service that puts me off: 'With all my leisure time I thee endow.' That's the bit I can't take."

Gazing now at the limply spreading figure of Alistair, she wondered whether Diana would be able to take it either, when it came to the point? If this long-drawn-out, low-key relationship were ever to to culminate in the conventional happy ending, wouldn't Diana feel exactly as Bridget about the sacrifices involved?

Must talk the thing through some time, she reflected. Not tonight, obviously.

"Where's Diana?" she asked sharply; and at this, signs of life began to quiver through the somnolent form before her. The eyes opened, a nondescript greeny-grey under the heavy lids, and the long supine figure coiled itself reluctantly into a sitting position.

"Where indeed?" he remarked pleasantly. "I've been waiting here for hours, and not a dicky-bird! No one tells me anything!"

"Was she expecting you?" interjected Bridget, as ungraciously as she dared. "We'd planned to have this evening on our own, you know."

"Ah well. The best laid plans of mice and men . . .!" He sighed and Bridget wondered, not for the first time, if he actually *wanted* her to throw something at him. Or did he really think that these remarks were funny?

Whichever it was, she didn't have to put up with it. He wasn't hers.

"Hasn't she rung or anything?" she snapped? "Something must have happened, because I know she meant . . ."

"My darling, *of course* something's happened. Things are happening all the time. All over the world. Didn't you know?

"*Alistair!*" Bridget was almost shrieking now in her impatience. "*Has* Diana telephoned to say what she's doing? Or hasn't she?"

"Yes *and* no, actually," he responded thoughtfully. "As is so often the case in human affairs . . . All right, sweetie, don't get so worked up! The answer is, yes, she did ring up; but no, she didn't say what she was doing. Or rather –" here he paused, perhaps to collect his thoughts, perhaps merely to annoy – "She didn't explain it so that anyone could understand. She seems to have been held up somewhere. Like at work. Or maybe at the hospital? Take your choice."

"*Hospital?*" For a moment Bridget was quite scared. Then she remembered: Diana had been due for one of her check-ups at the Infertility Clinic this afternoon. This was something else they were going to have to talk about before long. Her friend's notion that she would be able to carry on with her demanding job, as well as being a single parent, seemed to Bridget pure fantasy. And in any case, fancy *wanting* to have Alistair's baby! And not merely wanting it, but wanting it so passionately as to be undergoing weeks of poking and prodding, hormones, special diets and the rest.

Oh, well. At least it didn't seem to be working. Not so far.

But now Alistair was actually volunteering some information, unasked.

"Not to worry, my pet," he was saying, "She'll be back in her own good time, as always. And meantime, *I've* been holding the fort. I've been taking no end of messages from gibbering applicants for a share in this grotty flat of yours. No, dearie, I did *not* say "grotty" to them – as if I would! On the contrary, I made it sound like a cross between Buckingham Palace and a colour-spread in *Homes and Gardens*. They'll be along in droves. Any minute, I wouldn't be surprised." Here he yawned, stretched himself out into his former lounging position, and continued: "Actually, one little lady has been round already. I've interviewed her myself, isn't it lucky I don't make a charge for this sort of service?" Here he yawned again, and Bridget moved further into the room, tossing her scarf over the back of a chair and shaking loose her damp hair.

"Go on," she said. "Who was it? What's her name? What's she like?"

"Like? Well, the first impression I got was that she'd be just what the doctor ordered. Self-effacing to the point of non-existence. Pathologically anxious to please. Anxious altogether, I'd say – a genetically-programmed worry-guts. But that'll make her all the more malleable, won't it? And malleable she'll need to be, won't she, with you two harridans pushing her around?"

"How old? Oh, the sort of age women usually are these days – *you* know. What does she look like?" he paused, giving the thing careful consideration. "Well, like an earwig, really. Small, and scuttling, and giving you the feeling that it might be kinder to tread on her straight away and put her out of her misery. Ideal, I'd say, for a pair of heavy-hoofed ungulants like you two."

"'Ungulates', I think you mean," said Bridget icily. 'Ungulant', if there was such a word, would be the participle, not the noun . . ."

She stopped. There was something about Alistair which somehow forced her to talk like a tetchy schoolmistress, and she didn't like it; so she changed the subject.

"What time was it . . ." she was beginning, but Alistair interrupted.

"Oh, and another thing: didn't I say she was ideal? On top of everything else, she's a Battered Wife. She's on the run from one of those Refuges or something. Diana's going to love it! Didn't she say they'd be targeting Battered Wives for their next 'Can you Help?' programme? Madam Earwig should be God's gift to anyone like our Di, trying to claw her way up in T.V.'s compassion racket."

Alistair loved to make fun of Diana's job, and indeed it was a job that was easy to make fun of if, like Alistair, you were that way inclined. She worked on a newly-established T.V. channel, where she set up documentaries relevant to one or another of today's fashionable areas of concern: Hospital closures, abused children, dangerous dogs, satanic rituals, and, yes, battered wives. It wasn't she who chose the subjects – in general, these were handed to her by the programme-makers – but it was Diana's task to track down individuals who had suffered spectacularly from whatever happened to be the latest shock-horror cause of the day, and to prepare them for interview.

12

"What time was it when this woman . . ." Bridget was beginning, she stopped as she heard Diana's key in the door.

It must have stopped raining by now, for Diana's abundant bronze-gold hair fell in luxuriant waves to her shoulders without any hint of damp or dishevelment. It was a style perhaps a little too young for her thirty-seven years, but she was still just about getting away with it; probably would do for at least another two or three years. At the moment, she looked younger even than usual, her face flushed and eager, whipped into colour and freshness by the cold air outside.

"A drink!" she cried gaily, addressing her recumbent lover. "I'm dying for a drink, I've had a perfectly *awful* afternoon!" and now at last Alistair lumbered to his feet and set about making such a comfortable clink of bottles and glasses that even Bridget felt her irritable mood subsiding. Soon the little party were settled round the imitation coal fire (a very good imitation, as it happened) and Alistair was repeating, for Diana's benefit, the news about the putative new tenant.

"A battered wife, Di!" he repeated gleefully. "Isn't that what your coven of ghouls is working on right now? You'll be able to fatten her for the slaughter and dish her up oven-ready for the cameras without even stepping outside your own front door."

Diana laughed, happily. She always did when Alistair teased her, even when there was an edge to the teasing which some might have found hurtful.

"Good thinking," she responded: "But you know, Ali, it doesn't really work like that. You can't really use someone you know personally in this job. It's not ethical".

Ethical? Did that really bother these Media people? Alistair's mouth had fallen open in genuine surprise, but before he could frame a question to this effect, Diana had continued:

"Not that she'll be suitable, anyway, darling. Not as a tenant, I mean. A battered wife – she won't have any money, will she? We need someone who can pay a proper rent – that's the whole idea. No, it's impossible."

As she finished speaking, Alistair reached across from his low seat, caught Diana's hand, and planted a languid kiss on it.

'What a mercenary little maggot it is!" he chided her. "Anyone would think, watching these caring, sharing, soul-baring programmes of yours, that somewhere, deeply buried among the guff, there might be some idea of actually *helping* the victim you've got your claws into. Like, right now, if this earwig woman were to walk in, all bruised and bleeding from her latest set-to with hubby, and was to beg you on her bended knees for shelter – you know what you'd say? You'd say to her, "That's fine, my dear, that's absolutely great! Hold it! Don't move, stay on your knees, just the way you are. The head, though . . . just a fraction more to the left, if you don't mind. We want to see the blood running down your left cheek. Yes . . . that's right . . . That's absolutely fine . . . Hold it, dear . . .' That's how it would be, darling, wouldn't it? Admit!"

Diana laughed again, a trifle uneasily; but before she could think of a suitably light-hearted and jokey come-back, they were startled into silence by a ring at the front door. A small, tentative sort of ring it was, as if the visitor were unsure if she had found the right address, or unsure, it might be, of her welcome.

14

Chapter 3

"Earwig" was not a nice thing to call anyone, but all the same you could see what Alistair meant. Norah Payne was small and brown and compact, and there was indeed something insect-like about her swift, nervous movements. You were reminded of the instinctive movements of a creature for ever in the presence of larger, cleverer, weightier creatures, against whom the only protection lay in speed, invisibility and superior reaction-time.

A drink for the visitor? A comfortable chair? – and then the uneasy embarkation on a tenant-landlord interview – particularly uneasy in this case, because the landlord contingent already knew that their final verdict was going to be "No.".

Well, of course it was. It had to be. Anything else would be crazy: but this undoubted fact was not sufficient, alas, to prevent them feeling like heartless monsters. And every word of Norah's tale of woe was making them feel worse.

Nineteen years married (About forty, was she? Hard to tell from the dry, brown skin of her face, wholly devoid of make-up, and the lines of tension around mouth and eyes). Long-married, anyway, to this fan-tastically handsome man who had seemed, at first, like

15

every magazine-heroine's dream. He was tall and dark, with beautiful manners: the kind of man you were proud to introduce to your family and friends. Oh, and very, very rich . . .

Rich? Had that mattered so very much?

"Oh *no*, it wasn't the money", Norah hastened to assure them. "You see, it's not a rich man's money that makes him attractive, it's that gloss of success that radiates from him. It goes beyond good looks – beyond even a nice nature. Know what I mean?"

Did she know? Bridget wanted to deny it. Success – yes, and the gloss of success – was something she coveted for herself, not for any man in her life . . .

But it was necessary to concentrate. Norah was launching, now, on the harrowing story of her marriage: the violence, the threats of worse violence: the knives, the lighted matches, the drunken assaults . . .

"He's an alcoholic, then, is he?" enquired Diana, alert with professional interest. "You could have gone to Alcoholics Anonymous, you know. They have a special section for the relatives of alcoholics . . . We did a programme on them once, and it seems they are very helpful and supportive. If you like, I could give you an address . . ."

"Oh, *please*! Oh *no*!" Norah's hands, folded neatly in her lap, could be seen, if you looked closely, to be trembling slightly. "Oh *no*, I wouldn't dare do anything like that! Mervyn would kill me if he found out. And he *would* find out. He's always found out everything . . . that's why, in the end, I had to run away, there was nothing else I could do . . .

"And so that's how I ended up in this hostel for Battered Wives . . . I was that desperate . . . It seemed to be my only hope. But – you know what happened? Mervyn traced me! I don't know how he did it, I'll never know. He's a Consultant, you know, at a mental hospital; he has his ways. Anyway, there he was, early one morning, I saw him out of the window. So I snatched up the few things I'd brought, and climbed out of the window into the garden, and over the back fence into the road . . ."

"But, my dear, you didn't need to go to those sort of lengths," interposed Diana. "These refuges are specially planned, you know, to protect women from husbands who turn up like like that. They'd have kept him away from you, really they would. Actually, I've been involved in a bit of research about the battering syndrome, and I can promise you that . . ."

The quivering hands had grown still, brown and dry as dead leaves, and clutched together so tightly that they seemed no bigger than a cricket-ball. And now tears were beginning to trickle embarrassingly down the sallow cheeks.

Embarrassingly, because tears *are* embarrassing when you don't know the person well enough to put your arms round her. Or so it seemed to Bridget, who, in any case, was by now feeling a slight physical revulsion for the sad little creature cowering in the big chair.

Pretend not to have noticed the tears. Change the subject.

"Let me get you another drink" was the best she could manage, and headed for the kitchen, on the pretext of needing more ice.

Deliberately, she dawdled over her errand, gazing longingly at the lamb chops still languishing in the fridge. By now, she and Diana should have been enjoying them, together with mushrooms, tomatoes, cauliflower and mashed potatoes. Now it had all been spoiled; first by bloody Alistair, and now by this intrusive woman. A born victim-type, no wonder her husband beat her up – but before Bridget had time to examine this uncharitable and wholly unjustified assumption, she was interrupted.

"Bridget! What on earth have you been doing? Leaving me to cope single-handed all this time!"

Diana's hissed reproaches were justified, Bridget had indeed been dodging out of an awkward situation, and was ready – almost – to admit it.

"Sorry. I was thinking about those chops. I'm starving, aren't you? Why don't I start cooking while you get rid of the woman? Or, better still, get Alistair to do it. Time he did *something* useful about the place."

"Oh, but Bridget, *no*! It's Alistair that's the problem. He's saying things like: haven't I any compassion for a fellow-creature in distress? You know how he was going on about it even before she arrived, and it's worse than ever now she's started crying. Out loud, like a baby, and he's got her in a great compassionate bear-hug on purpose, just to show me how uncompassionate *I'm* being. I know that's why he's doing it, I can see his eyes peering at me triumphantly through those dried-up gingery wisps of her hair. He knows he's winning, he knows he's making me feel awful, he's doing it *on purpose*!"

Bridget agreed that he probably was.

"But, Di, you don't have to take any notice, you know how he is. He loves to tease you, and anyway everything's just a game to him: I think that's why I get so fed up with him, and you should, too. Just take a firm line. Get him to give her a lift to wherever she wants to go. *That'll* exercise his compassion all right, especially if it's somewhere in South London."

"But that's the whole point, Bridget. She *hasn't got* anywhere to go. That's why she's here. She thought, you see, that anyone advertising a room to let would at least *have* a spare room, and could let her stay in it for a night or two, just until they got a proper tenant. And of course we *could* do that. As Alistair says . . ."

"To hell with what Alistair says! It's what *we* say that counts. And so long as we back each other up saying 'No' . . ."

"She wants to pay us," Diana interposed tentatively. "She's not asking for charity, she says. She just wants . . . just for a night or two . . ."

"It won't be just a night or two! You know that as well as I do. Once she's here, there'll be no way of getting her out. There are actual laws we'd be breaking if we put her out on the street, never mind Alistair and his compassion. Talking of compassion, what about all those dozens of applicants he says phoned up this afternoon? Haven't *they* any rights, having applied before she did? And how does he know *they* aren't all cripples or mental defectives or something, and even more deserving of his precious compassion than she is?" She was being really nasty, she knew; but, Hell, she was so *hungry*.

"There weren't dozens, actually" Diana now admitted. "He says now that there were only two – and neither of them in the least bit crippled. One was an American fast-food executive wanting a pied-a-terre in London for the next six months while he organises a merger, or something. The other was a Yuppie sort of a

19

fellow who wanted to make sure there would be parking space for both his cars. Besides, as Alistair says . . ."

Bridget felt that if she heard even one more thing that Alistair had said, she might actually scream.

"Look," she said, "Let's just throw them out – both of them – and have our meal in peace. Neither of them have been invited – Alistair wasn't supposed to be coming again until Sunday, I thought you said."

She slammed on the gas, noisily filled a pan with water and set it to boil, then bent to light up the grill. Only now did she notice that Diana still hadn't responded to this tirade. Turning round, she saw her friend fiddling uneasily with the egg whisk and not looking up.

"Ye-es" Diana began guiltily, "I did say that, I know. But what's happened, you see, Bridget – I was at the clinic for my test results this afternoon, and they took my temperature – they do that, you know, it's routine – and it turned out to be a little bit up. Ninety-nine, that's all, nothing much, but enough to show that I must be ovulating right now, three days early. So I rang Alistair straight away to see if he could come tonight instead of Sunday. But I only meant the *night*, Bridget, honestly. It never occurred to me that he'd turn up early like this, in time for a meal and everything . . ."

Why hadn't it occurred to her? She'd known Alistair for six or seven years now, and for three of them they'd been lovers, surely by now she should be familiar with his wayward, self-centred ways? If it was convenient to him to arrive at the flat early, in time for an evening meal, then early he would arrive, serenely confident that a meal of sorts would be forthcoming.

It was Diana's fault entirely. How could a man *not* come to expect something that was invariably forthcoming? Even the Pavlov dogs had had that much intelligence.

What had the Pavlov dogs done when, on occasion, the expected meal wasn't forthcoming? This must surely have formed part of the experiment – Pavlov had been a painstaking and thorough researcher. Indeed, Bridget had a vague recollection of having read somewhere that the dogs had gone on salivating for a surprising number of minutes – 27.4 or something like that. Which meant (she glanced at her watch) that Alistair would still be salivating when everything was ready, the cutlets done to a turn.

He *wasn't* going to have any. He just wasn't. How could four cutlets be divided between three people? Bridget was the cook tonight, and the cook, always and everywhere, is the one with power. The power to inspire friendship, peace and contentment for a whole evening; also the power to wreck everything.

All power corrupts, absolute power corrupts absolutely. Disagreeable though she was feeling, Bridget did not fancy the idea of being corrupted absolutely, and so she sought a compromise. Couldn't they get Alistair to take this Norah woman out for a meal, dump her back wherever she came from, and then, if he had to, return to the flat?

Yes, he did have to. That was already clear from Diana's fraught expression and the increasingly nervous gyrations of the egg-whisk. The tiresome drama surrounding Diana's ovulation cropped up month after month: the arithmetic – the calculation of the exact night, almost the exact hour, when love-making (if

21

one could still call it that) would have the maximum chance of making Diana pregnant. Then there were the calculations – all the unpredictable variables – the hasty summoning of Alistair when the moment seemed ripe. It was irritating, but Bridget bore it as best she could. After all, Diana *was* thirty-seven, she couldn't afford to wait much longer for Mr Right to turn up; wiser, no doubt, to settle for Mr Wrong while she still had him. "Striking while the iron was hot", as Alistair himself would doubtless have put it, had he known what was going on.

But Alistair *didn't* know – or so Diana insisted. But was he really so stupid, Bridget sometimes wondered, as not to have put two-and-two together in respect of these periodic, urgent summonses to Diana's bed, especially considering the low-key, lackadaisical nature of their normal relationship. Or, on the other hand, perhaps he wasn't stupid at all, but fully aware of Diana's frantic manoeuvreing of their love-life, and secretly flattered by it? After all, for someone to be going to all this trouble to create a replica of oneself – it must surely be flattering on some level?

Whatever his attitude, Diana seemed undeterred by the problems.

"Men are funny about babies, you see," she'd explained one night when she and Bridget had both arrived home after midnight, and had sat talking in the kitchen instead of going to bed, "The human race would have died out long ago if it had depended on men agreeing to have a baby. So women have to take it into their own hands – since the invention of birth-control, that is. Men *always* want to put it off. Not now, dear, not till I've passed my exams. . . . settled into my new job . . . got the business back on its feet . . . got my promotion. And what about our lovely holidays abroad, darling, wandering free as air to any part of the world we like – how could we do *that* if we were lumbered with a baby?

"And finally, when maybe, in the end, he's come round to it – by that time the woman is too old. So, like I'm telling you Bridget, the survival of the human race from now on depends on women. It's a grave responsibility."

Grave indeed; and dependent, according to Diana, on women pretending to have taken the Pill when they hadn't . . . pricking holes in their female condoms . . . "All sorts of dodges" as Diana put it; and Bridget would listen, slightly perturbed, but in no position to argue. After all, she wasn't thirty-seven, and had so far experienced no maternal urges whatsoever. On the contrary, her feelings on the subject were virtually identical with those of the male sex as described by Diana. Not now. Not yet. I want to get on with my career. I want to enjoy my freedom.

Anyway, this was no time to get involved in such discussions. Prodding the potatoes with a fork, Bridget judged that they were just about done. The cutlets under the grill were beginning to smell delicious, and she was just nerving herself to march into the sitting-room and explain (as pleasantly as such a thing can be explained) that neither of the unexpected visitors were going to get anything to eat, when Alistair sidled into the kitchen with a plan of his own.

"We're going out for a takeaway," he said. "I've explained to our guest that in dealing with such a stingy, inhospitable pair as you two, it's the only –"

"*Inhospitable!* Oh, that's not fair!" cried Diana, cut to the quick. "Look at all the times when I've . . ."

"I wouldn't dream of looking at them" Alistair replied haughtily. "That would be looking at the past, wouldn't it? Only the Oldies look back at the past. I'm a Now-person. I live in the present. The Present is all we have, and if the present consists of two greedy, sef-indulgent harridans refusing to share their delicious meal . . ."

By now, just a little too late, Diana realised that he was joking, and she gave an appropriate little laugh.

Then, suddenly, she tensed up again and became serious.

"You *are* coming back, aren't you, Ali? For the night, I mean? It doesn't matter how late . . ."

He laughed, amiably enough, and chucked her under the chin.

"Of course I am, chicken! Wouldn't miss it for anything!" He laughed again, and winked mischievously at Bridget; making her wonder, yet again, if, perhaps, he *did* know what Diana was up to, after all? And was keeping quiet about it in order that, whatever happened, no one could possibly say it was his fault?

Chapter 4

It was after midnight when Alistair and his protegé
returned. Bridget had been on the point of falling
asleep when she was roused by the furtive opening and
shutting of the front door, followed by the hushed and
unnerving tumult that is characteristic of people trying
to be quiet.

Diana, as Bridget well knew, wasn't a deep sleeper
at the best of times, insomnia was more her style; and
on this night in particular, with thermometer, stopwatch
and menstrual chart all at the ready, she most certainly
wouldn't be sleeping.

So Bridget calculated; and swiftly following on this
thought came its comforting corollary; namely, that
Diana should be the one to get out of bed and cope
with whatever needed coping with. Organising the spare
bed (for at this hour there was no option *but* to allow
the woman to stay the night). Clean sheets, towels,
pillow-cases; making her a mug of something or other;
asking her what she liked for breakfast, and when she
wanted to be woken. Bridget lay very still, determined
to do absolutely nothing.

It was fair enough. The whole thing was Alistair's
fault; he was Diana's boy-friend, not hers. Snuggling
down under the duvet, feeling deliciously un-guilty

about sloughing off all responsibility for what was happening, Bridget was soon asleep. It wasn't until morning that she realised there was a price to be paid for this sloughing-off of responsibility. There always was.

For by leaving the whole awkward predicament to Diana, she had been, in effect, leaving it to Alistair, and ensuring that his impractical decisions would prevail. Diana would be sure to go along with whatever he recommended; and this, while Bridget slept, was exactly what came to pass.

Norah was to stay. Not just for this one night, but "Until she's got herself sorted out."

"And look, she's even paid a week's rent in advance!" proclaimed Diana, flourishing in front of Bridget's face a little clutch of bank-notes, for all the world as if they were a symbol of victory: when, in fact, as Bridget could see at once, they were a symbol of abject defeat.

Norah had won. She now had a *right* to be here. Not just for the one week, but for all the foreseeable weeks while the intricate and time-consuming legal complications of getting her out dragged on, and on, and on . . .

Bridget tried to convey her dismay and apprehensions to Diana, but with only partial success; for Diana was already in a hurry, pouring soya milk onto her muesli with one eye on the clock.

"Oh, but Bridget, she's not *like* that, I'm sure she isn't. She knows she's only filling in until we get a proper permanent tenant – and, let's face it, we haven't got one yet, have we? There's no harm in getting a little money while we wait – and in cash, too. I can't possibly get to the bank this week, and you know what a bore it is queuing up outside those cash-dispensers, and half the time they don't work anyway. Here, you have half!" – and she proffered the handful of notes spread out in a fan, like a deck of cards.

Bridget was about to refuse indignantly; then changed her mind and accepted. These notes, added to the contents of her own wallet, would enable her to return the whole sum to Norah, in cash, this very morning. That way, the whole transaction would be rendered null and void; surely it would? The thing would have to be done nicely, of course; no point in causing offence, and perhaps further fuss . . .

It was mid-morning, and the others had long left for work, when Norah, wearing the over-large flowered housecoat that Diana had lent her, made her way into the kitchen. The first thing she saw was Bridget's note, propped up against the electric kettle, so that she couldn't even make herself a cup of tea before reading it.

It was a nice enough note: ". . . welcome you here as our guest for a day or two . . . Couldn't possibly accept any money . . . Must have a proper talk this evening . . ."

Slowly, Norah put the letter back into the envelope, together with the spurned bank notes. She no longer felt like having a cup of tea, and so she wandered out of the kitchen, still clutching the letter and the money in a trembling sweaty hand. Catching sight of the winter sun pouring in through the big windows of the room where they had all been sitting last night, she moved into its quiet glow and settled herself in one of the deep armchairs that faced towards the windows. An expanse of sky confronted her, and a criss-cross of black twigs belonging to a tall tree.

She turned the envelope over in her hands once or twice, but didn't re-read Bridget's note. She knew well enough what it said. It said that she couldn't stay; not for more than a few days, anyway; at most, a week or two. Would a week – two weeks – be enough for her purposes? She must think . . . think.

The important thing was that they mustn't discover why she had come, nor where she had just come from. Insanity frightened everyone, and with reason – no one knew that better than Norah herself, which was why she must think so hard, and so rapidly. Before they all got back this evening, she must have decided exactly what she was going to tell them.

Unfortunately, she had already closed some of her options by what she had already told them; perhaps she had already made things worse for herself?

What had possessed her, for instance, to tell them that she had no children? The television woman, Diana, had pounced on it at once: Why, if she had no children, had she needed to go to a refuge at all? An independent, able-bodied woman like herself – why couldn't she have just walked out on her husband and found herself a job?

A good question. She, Norah, should have thought of it herself, and adapted her story accordingly. Obviously, she couldn't have told them about Christopher, because that would have involved telling them what had happened to him; but surely she could have invented some imaginary child? A little girl called Alice, perhaps, aged nine, with long blonde hair and learning the violin? Or a son about to take his degree in Modern History and hoping to get into publishing?

But the trouble with this sort of thing was the questioning that would follow. Why doesn't your son do something to help you? surely he's old enough now to stand up to his father? Or: How is it you've run away without your little girl? Surely you're not leaving her alone with her cruel and violent father?

And that was another problem: the way she'd made Mervyn out to be physically violent. He wasn't anything of the kind, He'd never laid a finger on her, and she knew he never would. He was a reserved, intellectual man, a consultant psychiatrist at the local hospital, and he had honestly tried to help her with her problems; at the beginning, anyway.

Much of her anxiety, he'd assured her, was due to an unresolved fixation on her father that had damaged her relationships with men, including, of course, himself. Because her father had been critical, he'd explained, she saw criticism everywhere, so that when he, Mervyn, tried to offer helpful advice, she twisted it into some sort of attack. This made her very difficult to get on with, Mervyn pointed out; she seemed unable to tolerate the ordinary give-and-take of normal human intercourse. This, he'd told her, was the reason she was having such problems with Christopher. He, too, was a male, and so it was inevitable that he would arouse his mother's unconscious fears.

"You can't expect a thirteen-year-old to cope with the distortions of reality that you introduce into your relationship with him," Mervyn had pointed out, in those early days, when the troubles had only just begun; and Norah, younger and less cowed in those days – had snapped back smartly:

"What do you mean, 'distortions of reality'? You

29

mean I'm mad, don't you? That's what you're saying
– that I'm mad!"

"That's not a word we ever use," he'd reproved her
gravely. "No one – no one at all – is any longer classified
as 'mad'. We don't admit of any such clear-cut category.
Let us just say that your hold on reality is – well – is a
little tenuous . . ."

"Tenuous". The word had angered her at the time,
and now, more than four years later, it still seemed
to add up to a devious way of saying she was mad.
She remembered rushing in to her next-door neighbour for reassurance, confident of receiving it in full
measure. She and Louise had long been in the habit
of conferring together over their respective marital
problems, and very soothing it was, for they always
took each other's side in whatever the argument might
be.

"Mad? My dear Norah, *of course* you're not mad!"
Louise had cried, as Norah had known she would,
"I've never heard of anything so ridiculous!" And
then, elaborating on this as they settled themselves
around Louise's kitchen table with their cups of instant
coffee, she continued: "They" (meaning *men*, of course,
and husbands in particular) "They love to say that sort
of thing, just to boost their own egos. It makes them
feel grand, you see, to be the one *without* the failing
in question, whatever it is. After all, your Mervyn *is*
a psychiatrist and so he has to keep reassuring himself
that he's the pillar of sanity in a mad world. Desmond's
the same actually, only in our case it's about money, not
sanity. It's considered my wifely duty to be the little
pea-brain who can't understand figures and is madly
extravagant. When actually *he's* the one who keeps

exchanging cars and buying new Hi-Fi equipment, even if he is a financial adviser."

Norah, feeling better already, murmured her sympathy and whole-hearted agreement. The diagnosis seemed to be spot-on; at this stage of the problem, anyway.

But what, the two of them then asked each other, could you *do*? Argue back? Point out that you had bought your winter coat at a jumble-sale? That you had recently been complimented by your boss on the clarity and conciseness of your reports – hardly the kind of accolade to be awarded to a mad-woman?

Or should you, Louise mused, take the thing in your stride and let the husband get away with it? This way you at least ended up with a contented spouse, aglow with self-approval – surely an easier creature to get on with than one racked by guilt and self-doubt?

"And especially if he's a psychiatrist," Louise speculated. "Being in the right when everyone else is in the wrong is an essential tool of his trade, like a tractor is for a farmer. Take it away from him and he's had it. In his heart he knows this, and that's why he's so touchy . . .

"If I were you, Norah, I'd let it ride, I really would. Take it as a joke. Say something like: 'Oh, well, we're all mad these days, and can you wonder, with this Government?'"

But Norah and Louise had not gone into the political situation in that cosy chat four years ago. They almost never did, so engrossed were they in their own concerns. It had been fun, though, Norah remembered. She and Louise always had fun when they got chatting, even about their troubles. *Especially* about their troubles,

31

you might say. Until, that is, the real darkness set in; the real, escalating terror, which could not be confided even to Louise.

The sun had shifted by now, and Norah shifted with it, moving across the room and resuming her vigil at the end of the divan with its bright scatter-cushions, which caught the winter light invitingly. Not that she could see their glowing colours once she was sitting among them, but in a funny way she still felt their quiet welcome into the sun.

Maybe she was going to be allowed to stay after all?

Chapter 5

Bridget felt rather mean, going away for the weekend like this, leaving Diana to cope alone with this Norah woman, who was still there.

Not that there was any real reason for Bridget to feel guilty. She herself had taken no part in the decisions which had led to the wretched woman being allowed to land herself on them. She had been against it right from the start. She had seen the danger of being stuck with Norah, and to avert it had been prepared to stick her neck out and be the mean-spirited, ungenerous, un-compassionate one who had the nerve to say "No". The fact that compassion had prevailed – if indeed it had been compassion, not weakness on Diana's part, and sheer mischief-making on Alistair's – was nothing whatever to do with her. So what could be more right and reasonable than that Diana and Alistair should be the ones left to cope with the consequences of their own virtue? Do-gooders would get more respect, Bridget reflected, if they were faced more often with the actual consequences of the good they had done.

Watching the Essex countryside surging past the windows of the Inter-City train, Bridget made further excuses for her defection by recalling that this wasn't an impulsive jaunt in pursuance of her own pleasure, it was a duty, a rigid item in her time-table, fixed many weeks in advance. She made it a rule, in her busy and absorbing life, to find time for a visit to her parents not less than four times a year, not counting Christmas. It was an effort; but, like every other kind of effort, it became easier once you'd made up your mind that you'd *got* to do it, that there was no option. Once you allowed the slightest flexibility into the situation, the strain of it all automatically doubled. You found yourself burdened not only with the task itself, but with the having to decide whether to do it or not; you had to wrestle with your conscience as well as enduring whatever needed to be endured.

How long was it since Bridget had actually *enjoyed* being at home? As a child, she'd been happy enough. There'd been lots of things at home which had been fun: the swing in the garden; the family tortoise, who reappeared so faithfully with the returning sun. There had been the old apple-tree, too, with its twisted branches among which she would sit, absorbed in a book, for whole summer afternoons. Indoors, too, there'd been plenty to do, lots of books and toys, and a mother whom, as a child, she had loved devotedly, and who had always been extremely good company.

Even so, looking back over her school-days, she couldn't remember a time when she hadn't preferred term-time to holidays; weekdays to weekends. Certainly, by the time she went to Cambridge, Bridget used to set off at the beginning of each term with a heart singing with joyous excitement; and had returned home for the vacations with a sort of dulling of the spirit; a sense of life having come to a temporary standstill.

Perhaps all this was normal? Perhaps this was how growing-up was for everyone?

Sad, though. She thought of her father, waiting lovingly in the car-park, anxiously scanning the little crowd emerging from the small country station that served the market town to which he and her mother had retired. It would be almost dark by the time she arrived. Already the vast East Anglian skies were darkening beyond the speeding windows, and little scattered lights were coming on here, there and everywhere.

In less than ten minutes she would be there. Irrationally – indeed quite idiotically – she wished she had taken one of the slow, infrequent local trains, stopping at every single station, instead of this insurgent monster, swallowing up the distance, and with it her last minutes of solitude, at such unconscionable speed.

"Lovely to have you back, darling," her mother was saying, gesturing vaguely with the teapot to offer a second cup of tea without interrupting the conversation.

"Do have one of Mary Foster's mince pies. She made them specially and brought them in when she heard you were coming. They're nice and hot still."

The plate of mince pies as well as the tea pot were now swaying tentatively a few inches above the table, and Bridget felt constrained to take one of the bulging little things, though normally she never ate anything at tea-time.

"How nice of her," she said politely, taking a reluctant bite, and wishing she could remember who on earth this Mary Foster might be. These visits home would be much more interesting if her parents hadn't moved from the comfortable North London suburb where Bridget had grown up, and where several of the children she had once played with were still living as adults, and could be visited in their various homes. Most of them, of course, were married by now, a fact which her mother never failed to point out – very, very lightly, and looking painstakingly away from her daughter as she said it. All the same, news of these old acquaintances would have been marginally more interesting than news of these Mary Fosters and suchlike: the new neighbours of whom Bridget knew absolutely nothing, and about whom she could not bring herself to take the smallest interest.

It was the same for her parents, she suspected, when (in response to their eager request to hear news of "What you've been doing, darling"), she actually tried to tell them about her life. About this morning's International Steel Manufacturers Conference, where she'd been interpreting for the Russian delegation. Dutifully, she racked her brains for some incident of the morning that might be mildly amusing – as well as comprehensible – to the uninitiated. The argument at lunch-time, for instance, about the gaffe made by the new Swedish delegate who had replaced dear old X . . .

How *could* they be interested, when they knew nothing about dear old X and his foibles? By the time she'd explained all this, the whole story would have become so long and so tedious as to be intolerably boring to both narrator and listeners.

Instead, at her father's insistence, she set herself to explain the basic objectives of the conference; and soon found herself bogged down in technical details about the world steel market which were far, far more boring even than Mary Foster's mince pies.

Thus she was about to stop, to spare them any more of this pointless pretence of listening, when she realized, with a little shock, that her parents seemed to be *interested* in what she was telling them. Far from being glazed with boredom, their eyes were bright with interest as they leaned towards her apparently taking in every word.

For a fraction of a second she was deceived by this, into feeling that contact had miraculously been generated in this unlikely area. But of course it was not so: she realised almost at once what it was that they were so pleased about.

What a clever daughter we've got, they were telling themselves. Just listen to the long words she's using! All these technical terms – all these statistics about millions and billions of pounds – all these foreign countries whose economic systems she seems to understand! How marvellously the education we struggled to give her has paid off!

Yes, this was what they were thinking. They didn't care about the steel market at all! A childish, irrational fury surged up in Bridget uncontrollably; it reached her throat, and she heard her own voice grinding to a halt.

Why? Why be enraged by the innocent and harmless pleasure they were taking in her discourse? Why did she have this sense of being insulted and belittled to the very core of her being? If they had merely been bored by her recital she could have accepted it, even have sympathised. But *this* . . .!

As always, her mother was the first to realise that something had gone wrong; also, as always on these occasions, she set herself to smooth things over. Very often, she did not know what had spoiled things, but it didn't matter because the smoothing technique was the same in every case, and indeed it quite often worked.

Beneath half-lowered lids, Bridget studied her mother's face as well as she could in the dull, pinkish glow from the heavily-shaded, low-slung lamp which was the room's only illumination. Strange how a civilization which with such labour, such ingenuity and skill, had at last succeeded in replacing the dim, guttering candles of the past with limitless floods of illumination at the touch of a switch – that it should have reacted to this crowning glory of light by adopting a fashion for the dimmest lights possible, obscured by the most opaque of shades, in living rooms all across the land.

Of course, it made faces look younger, up to a point. It was making Bridget's mother look younger right now, blurring the worry-lines around her eyes, and dimming the ever-encroaching grey in her mousy brown hair. It had been more chestnut when Bridget was a child, bright chestnut and shoulder-length, swinging in the sunshine as she'd walked Bridget to school; and earlier still, when she'd helped Bridget to rig up a tree-house in the old apple-tree. The tree-house hadn't worked very well, it had been much more comfortable just sitting among the branches without it: but, oh, it had been fun to make! And it had been fun, too, to lower a basket and then draw it up to see what exciting thing Mummy had put in it: sultanas, perhaps, or a couple of ginger biscuits, or perhaps even a Mars Bar.

How close they had been once, she and her mother! What had happened to that closeness? The swinging sunlit hair was gone, to be replaced by this dull bob, much more suited to a middle-aged woman. What else had gone? To be replaced by what?

Almost desperately searching for clues in her mother's anxious, dimly-lit features, Bridget saw one thing clearly enough: her mother was frightened. Frightened of *her*, the high-flying daughter to whom she could no longer relate, and whose present life-style was beyond her comprehension. Beyond her comprehension too was what on earth she had done to upset this prickly, inscrutable daughter in mid-conversation; but whatever it was, she was determined to put it right by her well-tried technique of changing the subject.

Bridget saw it coming.

"How's your friend Diana?" her mother asked tentatively, anxious, lest even this polite enquiry should turn out to be controversial.

As indeed it could have been, what with Alistair and the infertility treatments and all the rest; but Bridget set a hasty selection-process in motion and launched into a brief account of Diana's T.V. assignments, including the possibility of a programme on battered wives. Women everywhere are fascinated by battered wives, and Mrs Sadler was no exception; and so the tea-table conversation became relatively easy and pleasant for a while – though boring, alas, to Mr Sadler, who didn't see why, since he didn't batter his own wife, he should be expected to take any interest in people who did. It was like expecting a football-hater to listen to endless post mortems about Nottingham Forest and Arsenal.

He retreated, only slightly disgruntled, to his own domain, and the mother-daughter conversation shifted focus, in just the direction that Bridget had feared it might.

"And how's this boy-friend of hers, this Alistair?" the older woman asked; and Bridget, knowing already where this was leading, answered warily.

He was fine, just fine (not that this was what her mother actually wanted to know). And, yes, he still came round to the flat quite a lot; and, yes, he still seemed very fond of Diana . . . and here Bridget could see the crunch coming.

"He can't be all *that* fond of her," – Mrs Sadler was already looking away from her daughter and nervously fidgeting with the tea-things – "I mean, he's been coming around for two or three years now, hasn't he? Isn't it about time he said something about *marriage*?"

It was, actually; but Bridget wasn't going to admit this across the generation-gap. "Oh, but mother, it's not *like* that!" she protested. "Not these days. Girls of my generation – they just don't think like that any more."

They do, as a matter of fact, but why admit it? Especially in view of what was to come next.

"Because I've sometimes wondered," Mrs Sadler was continuing, her glance darting furtively around the room, from the brown velveteen pelmet to the brightly-polished fire-irons – anywhere except at her daughter's face – "I've sometimes wondered whether – actually – it's altogether Diana that he comes to see . . ."

There, it was out! No wonder her mother was scared to look her in the eye! Bridget struggled to control the angry words that were rising to her lips.

"This is the absolute, outside limit!" she longed to

40

say, "Trying to marry me off to every single man you ever hear of my meeting! You don't care what any of them are like, or how bloody awful and impossible they may be. You don't give a damn whether I could possibly ever be happy with any of them, all you care about is that I should be *married*. Just because all your friends' bloody daughters are married.

And now, to crown it all, you are hinting that Diana's vulgar, chicken-brained boy-friend might turn out to be my Mr Right! You don't know anything about him, and what's more you don't care! He could be Jack-the-Ripper, he could be half-dead of Aids, and you wouldn't give it a thought! Just so long as I ended up *married* to him!

Can't you see how insulting it is? All the needling and hinting about me not being married yet? Yes, I *know* all my old friends are married by now. I *know* that I'm twenty-eight, and that in less than two years I'll be thirty. I can do sums, you know: I'm the one that got a starred 'A' for maths, remember?"

But of course she said none of these things. What would have been the use? The whole subject had by now become a no-go area between herself and her mother, and both instinctively drew back from any threat of direct confrontation. Time was – when Bridget was only in her early twenties and the subject had not yet built up a head of steam – when the two of them could discuss the subject almost rationally.

"I can't understand, dear," Bridget remembered her mother pleading rather pathetically, "I can't understand what it is that has turned you against marriage like this. It's not as if Daddy and I had quarrelled a lot or got

41

divorced or anything. You had a *happy* marriage to look up to."

Hard to explain that it had been her parents' very contentment with their lot that had set their young daughter on so determinedly different a path. The prospect of dwindling into a person who could actually be *happy* in so narrow and restricted a life was appalling.

It had been impossible to explain this to her mother at the time: it was even more impossible now. Bridget racked her brain for some innocuous subject to which she could deflect the conversation, uneasily aware that her mother's brain, across the tea-table from her, was engaged on a precisely similar quest. Two brains whirring in unison, scouring the ever-diminishing range of topics that were neither hurtful nor controversial nor intolerably boring.

It was her mother who spoke first.

"I thought perhaps this evening we might . . ." she was beginning warily: but before the uninviting project (whatever it might be) had been fully enunciated, there was a merciful interruption.

The telephone. It was the older woman, perhaps powered by more intense anxieties, who got there first.

"*Who*?" she said in bemused tones; and then "Yes . . . Oh, yes, of course . . ."; and then turning back into the room, rather wide-eyed:

"It's for you, dear," she said anxiously. "It's Diana. She seemed . . . Oh dear, I do hope nothing's *happened*!"

You mean nothing that will make me curtail my visit, Bridget commented silently, and picked up the receiver.

"Oh, Bridget! Thank goodness I've caught you! I was

afraid you mightn't have arrived yet, and I couldn't
possibly have left a message, it's just too awful. It's
Norah, you see, she's had some sort of a brain-storm,
it's absolutely terrifying. I just don't know what to do.
I hate to ask you to cut short your visit, but I'm really
scared, and Alistair says . . . ."

Chapter 6

Lying in bed some hours later in her old room, where the Famous Five books and her collection of glass animals still adorned the shelves over the desk, Bridget wondered uncomfortably whether she should have responded more promptly to Diana's urgent summons; should have snatched up her suitcase and dashed off to catch the next – and probably last – train to Liverpool Street. It would have been easier in a way, as well as kinder, because her suitcase hadn't even been unpacked yet. And maybe it would have been no more distressing to her parents than the present arrangement; that she should go back first thing in the morning instead of staying for the whole weekend as planned.

"Of course, dear, if it's an emergency," her mother had said with a lack of reproach which made Bridget feel even more guilty than she had in the first place. "The only thing is, dear, I don't like to ask your father to get the car out again, at this time of night. He's just getting over this cold, you see, and . . ."

And our whole evening will be disrupted, she could have added, and the special meal I'd planned will be spoiled. The chicken is in the oven already – it's a free-range chicken, I got it specially . . .

It was this latter, unspoken, part of the protest that

45

had decided Bridget. Her mother was a wonderful cook, the bread-sauce would be out of this world. It would indeed be a shame to miss one of the delicious meals which were the sole bright spots of these visits home. And Diana *did* tend to exaggerate things, didn't she? Surely the morning would be time enough to sort out whatever had been happening?

Bridget turned her head on the pillow to peer at the old-fashioned tin alarm-clock, with its phosphorescent hands, which had been a birthday present when she was eleven. Her mother always set it going for these visits, quite superfluously, because Bridget's digital watch was always on her wrist, guaranteed to keep perfect time for just about as long as it would take the world's population to double. But of course her mother could not be expected to realise this – or, rather, to take any notice of it – and thus deprive herself of the silly little ritual.

The insistently ticking little anachronism *could* be useful on occasions like this, when insomnia had taken its hold, and you wanted to watch time passing without having to raise your wrist to the level of your eyes.

Quarter past one. By now, presumably, the crisis at the flat would have been resolved, in one way or another. It couldn't have been that much of a crisis actually, not when you thought about it rationally.

Fixing her eyes on the dim square of her bedroom window – through which she had once imagined herself climbing, like the girls in the school-stories, to take part in some midnight feast – Bridget went over, in as much detail as she could recall, exactly what it was that Diana had told her about this brain-storm of Norah's – if that's what it could be called. What it had all amounted to, as

46

far as Bridget could make out, was that Diana, from the hallway, had been eavesdropping on a phone call of Norah's which had sounded "completely mad".

"No, Bridget, I don't know who she was talking to, but that's not the point. For all I know, she wasn't talking to anybody. The point is, she was hallucinating, talking about centipedes crawling out of the telephone into her ear. They were giving her messages for the King of the World – tapping out Morse code with their hundreds of legs – that sort of thing. She's mad, Bridget, she's absolutely mad. I'm terrified of being alone with her for the whole weekend."

Alone? What about beastly old Alistair? Couldn't he make himself useful just for once? Come around when he's actually wanted, instead of endlessly coming when he isn't?

"Oh, but Bridget, you don't understand! He's got all sorts of things to do this weekend, he told me. I can't ask him to come round specially . . . not after last Sunday. You see . . ."

Bridget did see. She saw all too well that Alistair's convenience must ever have absolute priority over anyone else's. It all added up to just one more illustration of the speciousness of that damaging proverb: "To understand all is to forgive all." On the contrary, the more clearly you understood your friend's silly reasons for doing the silly thing she is doing, the more impatient you felt with her; not in the least more forgiving.

"Well, *I'll* phone him, then," Bridget had retorted. "The whole thing is entirely his fault in the first place, and I'll damn well make him see that . . ."

"Oh, Bridget. Oh no! Don't do that! He knows about it already, you see, he was here when it happened –

we'd both just come in. But he thinks it's *funny*! 'My dear girl, we're *all* mad,' he said. 'The whole world's mad, why should you expect Norah to be different?' And off he went, laughing. I heard him laughing all the way down the stairs. No, Bridget, *please* don't phone him. It'll only make things worse."

It would, too. Alistair specialised in making things worse. Within this rather unpromising area of agreement, the discussion ground to a halt, with Bridget promising to return as early as possible the next morning. She'd made a few consoling remarks, of course, before ringing off. Such as that Norah might have been using the phone to tell a bedtime story to her absent child . . . Oh, all right, she hasn't *got* a child: her small nephew, then – *anything*.

"One thing you can be sure of, Diana, if you go around eavesdropping on other people's telephone conversations you're bound to get hold of the wrong end of the stick most of the time. Especially if you've only eavesdropped on one end of the conversation, the way you did. You say yourself that the woman's behaving quite normally now. Well, *you* behave normally too, and stop panicking. We'll sort it all out tomorrow – O.K.?"

Not entirely O.K.; but nevertheless on this unsatisfactory note the phone call petered out, and Bridget was after all able to enjoy the roast chicken, roast potatoes, roast parsnips, brussels sprouts and the famous bread-sauce with a clear conscience.

Well, fairly clear. Setting off next day into the mild, misty November morning, Bridget braced herself to face her parents' reproachful sadness at her precipitate departure; and it was only at the very last moment, when she turned at the garden gate to wave to them, that she realised, with something very like shock, how happy they both looked. You could almost imagine them closing the front door and executing a little dance in the hallway, from sheer relief.

Could it be – could it possibly be – that these duty visits were every bit as much of a burden to them as they were to her?

Lovely to see you, darling, Come again as soon as you can. All that sort of thing. Was it just a pack of lies? Or was it, more mysteriously, a fixed and unstoppable ritual that was becoming *more* important, not less, as it deviated further and further from anyone's real feelings?

Suppose they all decided to be honest with each other? Suppose her parents were to say to her one day: "Look, Bridget, let's face it: we all hate these visits of yours. You are bored to death by our humdrum ways, and we are terrified of this severe, high-powered person you've turned into. So let's pack it in, shall we? Let's decide not to see each other any more, ever."

How would she feel, if this were to come about?

Shocked. Shocked to the very core, as by an earthquake or by the declaration of nuclear war.

What price honesty, then?

Chapter 7

Norah had had no idea, of course, that her phone call had been overheard. Bridget, she knew, was away for the weekend visiting her parents, and she'd supposed that Diana and Alistair were still out, not having heard them come in. Indeed, if she hadn't thought herself to be safely alone in the flat, she would never have dared to make the phone call at all. It was a risky thing to do in any case, she'd known that all along, and had hovered for some time by the telephone table, wondering which was the most frightening – to phone or not to phone? She dreaded what she might hear; but, on the other hand, she *must* find out, somehow, what was going on in her absence. How were they managing? What, so far, had happened?

Trying to control the trembling of her fingers, she finally dialled the dreaded number, and waited.

What would she hear? Was she to be dragged back into that macabre and distorted world which was beyond her comprehension, but in which she would be forced to play her allotted part, as she had been forced to play it for so long?

Forced? Yes, it felt like being forced, though Mervyn continued to insist, with all the weight of his psychiatric qualifications behind him, that she had in fact chosen this awful distorted world herself, in preference to the real world; that she created it as an area within which she could deploy her neurotic symptoms with impunity. Her fear of the dark, for instance; her increasing agoraphobia, her phobia about inviting people to the house. It was this last which, Mervyn claimed, was the most damaging – to herself, to their young son, and, of course, to himself.

"What sort of effect do you think it's having on my career?" he'd demanded "Never feeling free to invite anyone home – never giving dinner-parties for my colleagues – never having people in for drinks? People are beginning to wonder what's the matter with us, and I must say I can't blame them. I'm wondering myself."

How long ago had this particular tirade taken place? Hard to remember, for it was one among so many during these last few years. What *was* easy to remember, though, all too easy, was that evening, nearly five years ago now, when it had all started.

It had been April, she remembered, early April; a cold, bright spring evening, and still light, for the clocks had only just been changed, and they were into Summer Time. For the first time in months they would be having their evening meal by daylight, and Norah, bustling around the kitchen, had noted this prospect with mild surprise.

Summer on its way: how nice; and Norah still remembered the feelings of contentment with which she had peeled the potatoes, set the table, preparing for a pleasant, ordinary family evening. A typical family evening, you'd have said, in this prosperous suburb with its tree-lined streets and its well-appointed houses, each with its own garage. Father coming home from work;

mother busy in the kitchen, and the thirteen-year-old son upstairs doing his homework. Maths homework, as it happened. Christopher was exceptionally good at maths – was expected, indeed, to be taking his Maths A-Levels the very next summer, as his father proudly boasted to other, less fortunate fathers of merely average sons.

"Only thirteen, and they're putting him in for it!" he would exult. They're expecting him to do brilliantly, his headmaster tells me. His results in the Mocks were phenomenal. Just about 100% on every paper . . ."

Norah was pleased too, of course, by their son's exceptional talent: though in her heart she'd have been happier if he'd gone out and about more, had spent more time with friends. If only he'd ever made any real friends; but somehow this had not seemed to happen. He was not unpopular exactly, just uninterested in the company of other boys in his age-group. However, Mervyn had hastened to assure her that this was perfectly natural in a boy of such enormously high intelligence. "It's impossible for him to find any intellectual equals among his peers," Mervyn explained, "And so of course friendship is difficult for him. With an I.Q. of 150 or so he inevitably finds the companionship of ordinary boys boring and unsatisfying. Real friendship is only possible when there is a degree of intellectual parity between the individuals concerned. Without it, the more intelligent individual will inevitably find the other one boring."

Was this true? It must be, since Mervyn was a consultant psychiatrist and had studied these things in depth; but all the same, it didn't accord with Norah's own experience. She herself had friends who were unquestionably cleverer than her, and others who were less clever, but she found herself able to have fun with any of them, and enjoy rewarding relationships on all sorts of levels.

Once or twice in those early days she had confided to her neighbour, Louise, her concern about Christopher's lack of social life: but Louise, like Mervyn (though from a somewhat different standpoint) was inclined to pooh-pooh the problem.

"You don't know how lucky you are, Norah!" she'd laughed. "While the rest of us are worrying ourselves sick about our sons getting into gangs, up to goodness knows what kinds of mischief, there are you with a son who actually *likes* doing his homework, and who is actually *there* for meals at the proper time! Enjoy it while it lasts, my dear! Because, believe me, it won't last for long. In a year's time I predict, or at most two, you'll be as frantic as the rest of us about where your boy is and what he's getting up to with his scrofulous friends. You know – vandalism – drugs – trouble with the police. You name it, the rest of us lie awake worrying about it, and that's what you'll be doing too, Norah, believe you me! The time will come when you look back on this innocent phase of his as a golden age!"

And indeed such a time did come about for Norah; a time which fulfilled Louise's light-hearted prophecy in a manner more grim, more terrible, than either could ever have imagined.

But all this was still far ahead. On that April evening, with the long summer daylight already in the offing, Norah was not experiencing any serious qualms about her son. He'll grow out of it, she was telling her-self, as one still can when a child is only thirteen.

He'll grow out of it, I'm sure he will, just as Louise says . . .

Half past six.

She heard her husband come in, as usual at this hour, and, as was his wont, he immediately made his way upstairs to his son's bedroom to gloat over the advanced nature of the work on which the boy was engaged.

Yes, to gloat. It always seemed to Norah that this was the only word appropriate to her husband's air of triumphalism as he came down the stairs from these sorties, glorying in the complexity of whatever problem was in the process of being solved. Mervyn's very soul seemed to be revelling in the child's mathematical precocity, basking in it to a degree that Norah sometimes found almost unnerving. Sometimes even embarrassing, though there seemed no point in saying so.

On this particular evening she had listened, as usual, to Mervyn's encomiums on their son's progress, and had duly said, "Yes, I see, how nice. Tell him supper's ready, will you?" She had gone ahead with dishing up whatever it was that she'd cooked. She couldn't remember, after all this time, what the meal was, though all the other details of the evening were burned into her mind indelibly.

For Christopher wouldn't come down. Twice he was called, first by one parent and then by the other, until finally Norah went upstairs herself to hurry him up.

It wasn't homework he was doing, she could see that at a glance. He was sitting, head bent, at the sturdy oak table which had been placed under the window specially for his studies, and he was so absorbed in his task that he seemed not to notice his mother's arrival, even when she came close up behind him. His back was towards her, and his fair hair, touched to pale gold by the last of the sunshine, hung over a forehead furrowed with indescribable urgency as he wrote and wrote, as if under threat of some approaching deadline. So small and cramped was the handwriting that at first she could make nothing of it, except that it consisted not of words but of lists of figures.

"What *are* you doing, Chris?" she asked, and this time he did seem to have heard her. He responded by hastily covering the page with his left arm and peering sideways up at her. She had never seen that furtive sideways slewing of his eyes before, and it was frightening. Someone else, someone she didn't know, was looking out of her child's eyes.

"Chris," she said again, and this time there was a note of fear in her voice. "What are you *doing*?" She added, as if to reassure herself that everything was normal, "It's suppertime, you know. You must come on down. You can finish that afterwards."

"What do you mean, *finish* it?" he demanded. "Can't you see it's the seventeen-times table? 'two seventeens are thirty-four, three seventeens are fifty-one, four seventeens are sixty-eight . . .'" Abruptly the sing-song recitation came to a halt, and once more he turned upon her that strange, sideways look. "Everyone will tell you that the seventeen times table can't be finished, that it will go on to infinity. But it won't. It *will* stop somewhere, and I have discovered a way to find out where. I am about to discover where numbers stop. I am the only mathematician in the world who can do this."

Completely baffled, and with a sickening kind of fear rising in her throat, Norah tried to bring the child down to earth.

"Come along," she urged him, and laying her hands on his thin, childish shoulders, she yanked him out of his chair and marched him to the door. "Everything'll be getting cold, so come on down and stop talking nonsense."

He came downstairs meekly enough, and he also stopped talking nonsense. In fact he didn't talk at all throughout the meal or for some time afterwards.

At that time – nearly five years ago now – Norah had still been in the habit of consulting her husband about any problems concerning Christopher. Well, why not? Mervyn was not only a concerned and caring father, but a psychiatrist into the bargain. And so, that evening, after Christopher had gone to bed, she told Mervyn of her anxieties, describing to him what she had seen.

"The seventeen-times table – on and on right up into the hundreds of thousands – I mean, what can be the *point* of it? It worries me. It looks, – I mean, don't you think? – it looks a a bit – well – obsessional? Oughtn't we to take him to see someone?"

It seemed to Norah that her husband's face had grown pale as he turned to face her from his desk, but his expression did not change. The light from his angle-poise lamp lit to full advantage his handsome, strong features; they shone out bland and unruffled as they always did when he was dealing with patients. This was his professional look, his stock-in-trade for dealing with other people's problems. A necessary one – so one was given to understand – in order to avoid *involvement*. Never, according to established psychiatric wisdom, should the therapist allow himself to become emotionally involved with his patient's problems, no matter how urgent

57

or traumatic these might be. He must dispense succour from outside like an international aid organisation, getting supplies through to a beleaguered population neutrally, without taking sides or making judgements.

Well, fair enough; professionalism was no doubt essential; but this was his *son* who was under discussion. Couldn't he allow even a flicker of concern to cross his face?

Yes? No? For some seconds he remained silent, watching Norah closely. Then, still without any change of expression, he spoke:

"My dear Norah, you really must try to control these maternal anxieties. The boy is growing up, he's not a baby any more. This mothering instinct of yours is beginning to get out of hand. It's going to do him real harm if you aren't careful. He's thirteen years old – and an exceptionally brilliant thirteen-year-old at that. He doesn't need your guidance any more – and particularly he doesn't need it about mathematics."

Norah cringed and hung her head at the jibe, but did not answer; and Mervyn continued:

"For God's sake, Norah, what do you think *you* can teach him about mathematics? He's already at university level – the headmaster told me so himself. He's going to be the most brilliant mathematician since Isaac Newton. How can you imagine that *you* are in a position to criticise whatever mathematical theory he may be working on – something far, far beyond your intellectual scope – and mine too, of course, but at least I have the sense to recognise my limitations."

At this Norah – braver in those early days than she could possibly dare to be now – stood her ground.

"It isn't a mathematical theory he's working on," she insisted. "I told you – it's the seventeen-times table, going on and on and on. There *can't* be any sense in it – especially since he's got that super-expensive calculator you bought him. If he wants to know what seventeen-times-something is, all he has to do is . . .

Expression had come over Mervyn's features at last. She was aware of a mounting tension in him, overlaid with a veneer of withering scorn.

"A typical Norah-ism!" he sneered – and she could tell that he was struggling to convince himself as well as her. "You haven't the faintest idea of what a calculator can and can't do, and yet you have the nerve to make these judgements! Calculators don't extend to infinity, you know; Christopher's onto something important there, because actually there's no such thing as infinity, it's just a mathematical abstraction."

She realised clearly enough that, deep down, he was as scared as she was by Christopher's aberration; but now, suddenly, his face cleared. He had thought of something.

"Hasn't it occurred to you," he exclaimed, "That seventeen is a prime number? Research into the nature of prime numbers is something that has engaged the minds of top mathematicians for centuries. Obviously, that's what Christopher is working on. It may be – I'm sure it *will* be – that our son is destined to be the genius who will finally solve the problem."

Mervyn turned back to his work with an air of over-whelming relief, and the uneasy exchange was over. The problem of prime numbers – whatever it might consist of

– was serving as a comfortable substitute preoccupation for the problem of Christopher's mental state.

And thus it remained for the following weeks, during which Norah's anxieties slowly and steadily deepened.

Chapter 8

By the time Norah had finished her phone call, relieved rather than dismayed by what she had heard – centipedes which tapped out Morse signals with their hundred legs were a soft option compared with the thing she had feared – it was quite dark. She drew the heavy, floor-length curtains against the misty darkness outside, and then sat for a while, considering her next move. They didn't seem to be thinking of throwing her out – not just yet, anyway; though it was awkward that they weren't letting her pay any rent. It made things embarrassing which would otherwise have been easy and straight-forward. For instance, right now she was wondering if she was entitled to switch on the imitation coal fire in this apparently communal living-room. Must have a talk with Diana when she comes in, she mused; and even as the thought passed through her mind, it was borne in upon her that Diana was already in, was, at this very moment, coming into the room.

But how strangely she was behaving! Pushing the door a little way open, and peering cautiously round it, as if fearing that something might be about to leap out on her.

"Hullo!" Norah said in what she felt to be a perfectly normal voice, and was about to continue with some sort of apology for having used the phone, and a promise to pay for the call, when Diana silently withdrew her head and retreated without a word, closing the door softly behind her.

It was a couple of uneasy hours later when the two met up in the kitchen, brewing respectively a mug of coffee and a half-pint packet of instant soup. With the to-ing and fro-ing in the restricted space around the cooker, unbroken silence was impossible to maintain; especially for Diana, whose curiosity had by now overcome her initial panic at finding herself locked up (well, sort of) with a raving lunatic, and who longed to hear more about the centipedes. Insane or not, it had to be a good story, and Diana was partial to good stories, both professionally and in her ordinary social life.

And so it came about that, within a very few minutes, the two of them were cosily seated one on each side of the imitation coal fire, sipping their hot drinks and embarking on that sort of late-night conversation which is bound to end in an exchange of life-stories.

Well, why not? Norah had realised, by now, that she was a very poor liar. Already she had forgotten exactly what she'd told her friends on that first evening. It certainly hadn't been a success; she'd already put her foot in it about that imaginary Women's Refuge – Diana had caught her out almost at once in some sort of factual slip. Even less did she remember what she'd told Alistair during that unexpected meal that she'd rather disconcertingly shared with him. They had had a pizza, and he'd ordered a bottle of red wine to go with it, it had been so long since she'd enjoyed the sort of social life that involved sharing bottles of red wine, that her two – or was it three? – glasses had gone straight

62

to her head, and her answers to his increasingly tactless questions had probably been wildly incoherent. Oh, she'd lied about herself all right, of that she felt sure: but even lies can be discreet or indiscreet. And anyway, he hadn't believed her, you could see he hadn't. He'd been amused, though, and she'd been hazily flattered to feel that she was still capable of amusing a new man, even after all these black years.

"I told you a lie!" she blurted out now, in response to Diana's cautious feelers. "I told you I hadn't got any children, but I have. I have a son. I didn't want to tell you about him, but I think I must. He's eighteen and he's a schizophrenic. I can't bear it any more and so I've run away, which was an awful thing to do. There, now you know. I'm bad news. Throw me out if you like, I wouldn't blame you."

She wouldn't, of course, be thrown out: no way. All unwittingly, she was employing the time-honoured Scheherazade technique: dangle a fascinating unfinished tale in front of someone, and rather than miss the dénouement they will refrain from murder, let alone from evicting you from their flat.

"It all began five years ago", she told Diana. "It was one evening early in April. He was thirteen at the time . . ."

But *was* that when it began? Hadn't there been earlier occasions – much, much earlier, when it could be seen, with hindsight, that something was wrong? Norah recalled her small son's perennial reluctance to spend time with children of his own age. It had been a nuisance, she remembered thinking, because it meant she couldn't join easily in the casual child-swapping arrangements by which the young mothers of the neighbourhood secured stretches of child-free leisure for themselves, turn and turn about; but it hadn't occurred to her, at the time, to worry about it. Nor did she rate as anything more than an inconvenience Christopher's tiresome tendency to ignore any child who had been invited in to play with him. After a few minutes of eyeing the newcomer in sullen silence, he would turn away and get on with his own solitary amusements, while his mother was landed with the task of entertaining the small visitor. Again, a nuisance, but not, so far as she could remember, a cause for worry. And, of course, with Mervyn assuring her that it was all because their child was so brilliant, and Louise next door assuring her that kids were all a pain in the neck one way or another (if it wasn't that, it would be something else) well, between the two of them, they quashed any qualms she might have had almost before they were born. And, on top of all this, Christopher was a very easy child in all sorts of ways; quiet, reasonable and well-behaved. She was lucky, really.

Or thought she was.

In the process of talking to Diana, it was all coming back to her with painful vividness; all the more painful because the events were now seen in the lurid light of hindsight; of knowing how it would all end.

"How awful for you," Diana was saying. "And so what happened after that?"

After the episode of the seventeen-times tables, she meant; and Norah tried to think. What exactly *had* happened next?"

Certainly, during the following summer, Christopher had become increasingly silent and moody – but wasn't that typical of adolescents everywhere? But there had been frightening episodes now and then. Norah recalled one that had happened in the summer holidays that year – August it must have been, late August. Christopher had spent the whole morning and afternoon buried in his studies; and Norah, having tried in vain to get him at least to bring his books out into the garden and get some fresh air, had finally given up and settled herself in a garden chair on the patio, from where she could see the late-blooming roses and hear the bees humming in and out of the michaelmas daisies. She was reading, deeply immersed in her book, and so wasn't sure quite when it was when the sound of hammering began, nor how soon it was when she began to realise that it wasn't one of the neighbours engaged on some piece of "Do-it-yourself," or "Do-it-your-selfishness," as Louise used to call it when it was her husband strewing sawdust all over the carpet. No, it wasn't a neighbour this time; the noise was coming from *her* house. Norah was at once pricked with unease, though she couldn't quite have said why. Surely it would be a *good* thing, not a sinister one, if for once Christopher had abandoned his books in favour of something practical?

She hurried indoors.

At first, she couldn't quite make out what he *was* doing. With hammer and nails he seemed to be fixing a huge wooden board, about two feet wide and five feet high, to his bedroom wall, while all around lay scattered chunks of plaster.

"*Christopher!*" she cried from the doorway "What are you *doing*? Where did you get that great piece of . . ."

And then she realised where he had got it. It was simply the reverse side of the full-length mirror which

65

had been a fixture on his bedroom wall ever since they'd moved here. With chisel and claw-hammer, he had wrenched it from its moorings, regardless of the damage to the wall, and was now savagely nailing it up again, with the glass facing inwards, against the wall.

"*Christopher*!" she shrieked, forgetting that she was a psychiatrist's wife, and giving way to blind fury, "How dare you! Just look what you've done!" – gesturing at the mess of scattered plaser.

And when he said nothing, paid no attention to her whatever, but just went on hammering, Norah plunged across the room, snatched the hammer from his hand, and demanded an explanation.

All this was entirely the wrong thing to do, as Mervyn was to point out in no uncertain terms when he arrived home that evening; but at the time it had seemed to be what anyone would have done.

And indeed, more or less, it had worked. It at least got the boy talking, giving a careful and considered explanation that, unless you had been listening closely, might have made his bizarre action seem almost sane.

"I don't like that mirror," he said, eyes narrowed. "I've never liked it. I don't like that boy who lives in it. I don't like the way he looks at me, sometimes he seems quite mad. He has mad eyes. He's always there, getting in the way, when I want to look at myself, and so I've decided to give him a lesson. He'll just be looking out at a blank wall now. That'll teach him!"

Diana was listening, rapt and spellbound, as indeed anyone might be.

"Whatever happened then?" she asked. "I mean, when your husband came home? Surely he realised then that the boy was mentally ill?"

66

"But he didn't, Diana. You won't believe it, but he still didn't. When he saw what had happened, the mess of plaster and everything, he was furious, of course, as anyone would be. But not with Christopher. No, with *me*! "Look what you've driven him to!" he said later that evening. "It's this crazy possessiveness of yours! I knew, I knew things were coming to a crisis! He's at this vulnerable age when he needs above all a supportive and understanding background – and what happens? You, his mother, have mishandled the situation so grossly as to exacerbate his normal adolescent identity problems to a point where some violent resolution is his only option. In order to save himself he has to destroy himself symbolically; destroy, that is, his mirror image. And I'm afraid, Norah, that you bear a lot of the responsibility."

"And then he listed all the awful things I'd done to him, ever since he was a baby. How I used to hold him up in front of the mirror when he was only a few months old, so that he could play a game of smiling, laughing, waving his arms about and watching the baby in the mirror doing the same. All right, it was a game; all right, the baby appeared to enjoy it; but did I not realise how dangerous a game it was? Deliberately inculcating the illusion of being two individuals, not one? What sort of a mother is it, he asked me, who goes out of her way to force a split personality on her child when he is barely a year old?"

"But how unfair!" Diana expostulated. "I'm sure all mothers and babies play this game with mirrors at one time or another, and the babies love it. Why should Christopher be the only one who . . ."

"Yes, well, that's what I said, more or less, but of

course Mervyn wouldn't listen. And he accused me of damaging the child by reading him *Alice through the Looking Glass* as a bedtime story. Didn't I realise that it isn't a children's story at all, but a farrago of obscene symbolism aimed at perverted adults? By reading him such a book, I'd been building into his psyche a deeply-entrenched phobia about mirrors, which was now distorting what would otherwise have been the normal identity-crisis of early adolescence.

"He ended up kind of forgiving me, and giving me instructions for my future behaviour: 'The important thing now, Norah, is that you *leave him alone*. Stop fussing. He is working out his own problems in his own way. Just get off his back, and he'll be fine.'"

Was it altogether wise, Norah was beginning to wonder, to be confiding all this in her companion? She didn't really know Diana all that well, and what she did know – namely, that Diana had some sort of a job in television – was not entirely reassuring. Might she not, even at this moment, be planning how to use these admittedly colourful confidences for some future programme? Could she do this without the permission, or even the awareness, of Norah herself? Having no knowledge whatsoever of how programmes were put together, and having herself watched many a documentary in which personal problems of such hair-raising intimacy were aired that it was hard to believe that the subject had given valid consent – in view of all this, she found her hands actually trembling as she helped herself to more coffee. She envisaged the possibility that Mervyn might by chance switch on the set one day, and be confronted by the terrible and long-kept family secret being beamed out to an audience of millions. In a single moment his painfully-preserved illusion about his son's normality would be held up to the mockery of the world.

Norah could understand his attitude well enough – though understanding, as so often happens, was of no particular help. She understood that so much of his own ego had been invested in this super-brilliant child of his, that to discover the worm at the heart of all this brilliance would be an ego-shattering experience so fearful that he just wouldn't be able to take it.

And it would all be Norah's fault, that was for sure. The disasters brought about by Christopher's illness always had to be her fault. Because if they weren't *her* fault, then there *must* be something the matter with Christopher, and this was unthinkable in Mervyn's universe.

Like the day of the dinner-party – the last dinner-party she had ever dared to give, incidentally, thus laying herself open to her husband's reiterated accusations of being obsessionally inhospitable, never inviting people to their home "like other wives".

For some moments she wondered whether to tell Diana even about this. It had been so humiliating that she had never told anybody, not even Louise next door. But might it not, after all this time, be some sort of relief to share the memory with someone? Someone right outside her own neighbourhood, and yet interested, as Diana clearly was. She was leaning forward, eyes alight, all agog to hear more.

To hell with the risk of publicity! Why should she suspect this sympathetic and warm-hearted person of planning to betray her confidences? By now – it was

69

nearly two in the morning – they had moved on from coffee to white wine, and this too made the decision easier.

She would tell Diana about the dinner-party.

Chapter 9

Christopher was fifteen at the time, and Norah had
long realised that there was something very serious
the matter with him, though in the face of Mervyn's
repeated and professionally-backed denials, she hadn't
yet given a name to it. She remembered praying, as
she bustled about getting the party ready, that the
boy would be in one of his quiet, unaggressive moods
that evening. He hadn't been too bad lately. Apart
from being withdrawn and silent, and now and then
muttering inaudibly to himself, he had caused no overt
trouble for a number of days, and it seemed reasonable
to hope that his behaviour tonight would at least be
inconspicuous. Being quiet and withdrawn would be
more or less O.K., for everyone knew that adolescent
boys were painfully shy in the presence of adults. He
might even opt for not coming in to the meal at all.
This would save a lot of worry, as well as making
the numbers round the table more manageable. Three
couples had been invited – colleagues of Mervyn's,
with their wives. With Mervyn and herself there would
be eight – a better number than nine from every
point of view, even had the ninth been more of a
potential asset to the gathering than Christopher was
likely to be.

Norah had taken a lot of trouble over the occasion, for she knew that all the guests were, in one way or another, important to Mervyn's career. She'd planned a four-course meal, even though it was going to take all day to prepare, and she'd set the table with candles, vases of lilies, and glittering glasses for the three different wines that Mervyn was planning to serve. She had brought out the little-used canteen of wedding-present cutlery, and had polished each fork and spoon to a satisfying brilliance. When all was ready, some while before the guests were due, she stood in the doorway of the dining-room admiring her handiwork. The table looked lovely – she imagined the little gasps of admiration as her guests filed in.

And little gasps there were, though not the sort that she had envisaged.

The first thing she took in, as she led them all to the dining-room, was that the table no longer shone and glittered as it had when she last saw it. She took a few moments to grasp what had happened to those bright implements she had set out so carefully a few hours ago.

They had been *bandaged*. Each knife, each fork, had been carefully and painstakingly bandaged, round and round, along its entire length. There they lay, like so many injured limbs in a surgical ward. And the lilies, tipped from their vases, now lay on their sides atop a pair of oblong cardboard boxes. In case anyone might miss the funereal effect, a large cardboard lid had been propped between the two coffin-like boxes, bearing in multi-coloured crayon the words "MEMMENTO MORI"

"He can't even *spell* any more!" was the thought that flashed idiotically through her mind while the full horror of the scene slowly sank in. She couldn't even think how to run away, so she stood stock still, as indeed did everyone else, speechless and staring.

Mervyn recovered first – if recovery it could be called, in a man whose face was as white as paper and whose teeth were visibly chattering.

"Sorry about this," he managed to enunciate; and went on, his voice beginning to recover a semblance of professional poise and coolness: "Norah, dear, I think you had better go and lie down, while I see to things." And then, addressing the non-plussed company: "I'm afraid my wife hasn't been very well lately. You must forgive her."

But Norah heard no more. At his words, her power of movement returned, and she fled. Not to lie down, of course, but into the kitchen, from whence, come what may, the meal must be served.

How Mervyn contrived to "see to things" she never learned; but quite soon all sorts of willing hands were flapping around her in the kitchen, helping, hindering, doing their well-intentioned best, while into her ears poured a flood of remarks intended to console, plucked at random from the familiar repertoire of platitudes. "Never mind, dear," "It's the heat, you know." – and even that hoary old chestnut, "It could happen to anyone." Which it manifestly couldn't.

That night, Norah's career as an object of pity, a target for sidelong glances, began.

She did not reappear in the dining-room, how could she? And who would have expected it? Instead, as soon as everything had been dished up, and assorted hands

73

were carrying dishes here and there, mostly in the right direction, she fled upstairs, and found herself confronting a serene and unusually communicative Christopher, preening himself on what he had done.

"Too dangerous, you see, Norah, all those sharp knives and sharp prongs of forks. *So* sharp – they could have hurt themselves. So I decided to pre-empt the woundings by bandaging them all up beforehand. I mean, better safe than sorry. Prevention is better than cure – all that stuff. I was a bit late for some, I'm afraid, several of the forks were already dead. You've never seen anything so sad – a little pile of dead forks! Luckily, though, I came across a whole lot of white lilies, so I was able to give them a decent funeral . . ."

Too shattered to reprove or argue, or even to cut short this flow of deluded and terrifying nonsense, Norah just slumped onto the boy's bed and let him rattle on in this strange, high voice which wasn't quite his own. She queried nothing, not even his elaborate explanation of why he hadn't bandaged up the spoons as well as the forks and knives.

"The spoons aren't *sharp*, you see. It stands to reason they aren't a danger to themselves or to the others, so I left them alone. Well, it would have been *silly*, wouldn't it, to bandage a *spoon*!"

He gave a little laugh at the absurdity of the idea, and waited good-humouredly for his mother to share his amusement.

At last, the high-speed delivery of explanations and self-congratulations began to subside; and eventually the boy fell into a dull, semi-lethargic state that was not quite sleep. Meanwhile, Norah heard at last from downstairs the unmistakeable sounds of departure: footsteps back and forth: doors opening and shutting; and even the bright prattle of "Thank you for a lovely party" – a phrase so deeply ingrained from earliest childhood as to survive even a gathering like this.

And afterwards? The whole thing had been too embarrassing too traumatic, for an ordinary marital row. Norah and Mervyn were both very silent as they went about the aftermath of clearing up and preparing for bed. At one point, Mervyn had said: "We must see about getting you some treatment, Norah," but apart from this clear indication that he assumed her to have been the perpetrator of the catastrophe, he voiced no reproaches. Not that evening, anyway. Nor, during the ensuing days, did he follow up his own suggestion of getting "treatment" for his wife. Under such treatment (perhaps he had asked himself?), what might she not reveal to whatever therapist he decided to send her to?

She wondered, as the days passed, whether he had spoken to Christopher about the catastrophic evening; and, if so, whether he had given his father the same bizarre explanation that he had given his mother.

Probably not. Even in his most wildly irrational state, the boy seemed to retain some sort of subliminal awareness of what should be kept from his father, and what it would be O.K. to mention.

And so, what with Christopher being wary about what he told his father, and his father being wary about what he asked, they managed to set up between them a wall of incomprehension strong as steel and thin as glass, and to maintain it successfully through almost any hazard.

And hazards there were, in plenty as the months went

by. Christopher was managing somehow to continue attending school without bringing down on himself any dramatic reproofs or interrogations. Perhaps he deployed at school the same subliminal awareness as he exercised with his father, and so got through the days without any overt displays of insanity. His work, though, had drastically deteriorated, and this his teachers *did* notice. Distressed and anxious notes from class teachers would arrive, and also a note from the headmaster; all to be scornfully dismissed by Mervyn as the work of little minds baffled by an intellect far superior to their own, and one with which they were quite unable to cope.

Once, Norah had ventured to go and see the head-master herself, without Mervyn's knowledge; but this had produced such fury in her husband that she never ventured on any such initiative again. Though the headmaster had, in fact, been sympathetic and helpful, and ready to reinforce the view that the boy was going through an identity crisis not uncommon in adolescence, and might benefit from some form of counselling . . .

"Though of course, Mrs Payne, your husband knows much more about this kind of thing than I do, and if he feels that Christopher would benefit from some course of treatment, then of course the school will co-operate in every way it can – letting him off classes to attend his therapy sessions and so forth . . ."

She had imagined that Mervyn would be relieved rather then upset when he heard what the headmaster's reaction had been. After all, hadn't Mervyn himself diagnosed an "Identity Crisis" as an explanation of their son's odd behaviour?

But nothing of the sort. That Norah should have ventured to arrange an interview with the headmaster without consulting him, seemed to Mervyn such an outrage, such a reversal of professional etiquette, that his fury about this completely obliterated any consideration of the actual outcome of the interview;

"He *knows* that I'm consultant psychiatrist at St Elmo's Hospital! He must have thought it extraordinary that you, and not I myself, should discuss the problem with him. It's *not* a problem! Christopher is going through a perfectly normal adolescent phase. It's not a problem at all, and if it was, it would be for *me* to decide what to do about it, not for that chicken-brained nincompoop who knows nothing whatsoever about psychology! There is *nothing* the matter with Christopher, except that he is unlucky enough to have a mother suffering from an anxiety-state so severe that she smothers him to death with her phobias and obsessions. You hardly let him out of the house by himself these days – can you wonder that he rebels occasionally in the only ways that are open to him?"

It was true that Norah worried about Christopher going out of the house by himself. On one of the recent occasions when he had done so, it had been for the purpose of dropping, through every single letter-box, on both sides of the road, an invitation to a party at his parents' home that same evening. Quite an elaborate invitation, in exquisite though very tiny handwriting, with pictures of balloons and toys all round the edge. Having devised the card, obviously with considerable care, Christopher had contrived to obtain a hundred copies from the school photocopier, and had distributed them with carefree abandon.

A large number of invitations had, of course, arrived through the letter-boxes of people who did not know the family at all. They were, no doubt, puzzled, but in some cases sufficiently intrigued to decide to go along.

And so that evening, as Norah was settling down to the washing-up, there was a ring on the doorbell . . . and then another . . . and another. By nine o'clock, there were something like fifty people crammed into the sitting-room, with a tin of biscuits and two half bottles of sherry between them.

"I'm afraid my wife is getting very forgetful," Mervyn kept repeating, as the first shock of the situation began to subside. "I had no idea that she'd planned this . . ." and with admirable poise and dignity, he'd urged patience on the assembly and had driven off at speed to the local wine shop, coming back laden with bottles.

Christopher, meantime, had been holding the fort at home, receiving the guests as if he was lord of the manor, bending his head to each, saying a few words and shaking hands. His fair hair, grown rather long of late, shone as it tossed back and forth on his forehead under the hall light. Norah, in the midst of her agonised embarrassment, had noticed suddenly how tall he had grown, and how handsome. No one would have dreamt, looking at him now, that there was anything at all the matter with him. Even Norah had found herself wondering, for one wild moment, if some miraculous recovery had suddenly come about?

But it hadn't. Day by day, things grew worse. Fired, perhaps, by the success of this first leafleting of the neighbourhood, Christopher plunged into an orgy of letter-writing, some of it far more offensive than an invitation to a non-existent party. Threats to sue over the barking of a non-existent dog were slotted through the street's letter-boxes one weekend: complaints about overgrown trees went to householders who had no trees in their gardens at all. Vague accusations of "insulting behaviour" went to people who had had no contact whatsoever with the writer or his family.

The neighbourhood, at first, had been fairly tolerant of these missives. After all, no harm was being done, and so no one lost anything by being polite.

"Practical jokes, that's all," they would say pityingly to Norah, pretending to believe it; "You know what kids are." A plausible comment, no doubt, had Christopher been seven years old. But he wasn't. He was seventeen now, coming up to eighteen. Almost a grown man. Already a grown man in height, and in his burgeoning muscular power.

"And so you see, Diana," Norah concluded wearily, tipping the last dregs of wine into her glass. "That's how it is, and I can't stand it. I just can't. I can't even speak to the neighbours any more, all of them knowing, and whispering about it. People are beginning to avoid me in the street . . . No one drops in any more. They're kind of scared, I know they are. Even my neighbour Louise – my very best friend – even *she* is cooling off. It was the last straw, I just *had* to do something. Didn't I?"

Chapter 10

"So it all turned out to be this Mervyn fellow's fault," remarked Alistair, having listened in, eyes closed, on the summary of last night's revelations. "But I don't see why you girls are so shocked about it. I thought everything was always the man's fault?" He yawned, stretching his long bulk even more luxuriously against the sofa cushions, and continued: "Isn't anyone going to pour me another cup of coffee?"

It was Diana, of course, who reached for the coffee pot, and Bridget watched the eagerly subservient movement with her usual flicker of irritation. Why couldn't the wretched man ever do anything for himself? The irritation, however, was a small thing – and she recognised it as such – compared with the enormous relief she was still feeling at finding life in the flat going on exactly as usual this Saturday morning. After Diana's panicky telephone call last night, and her own somewhat dilatory response to it, she had travelled back this morning in an uncomfortable state of guilt and unease. Suppose something awful really had happened at the flat in her absence? Suppose she'd arrived back to find her flatmate dead, or abducted, or in hospital, because of something that would never have happened if Bridget had rushed back as soon as she was summoned? She'd even felt relieved, as she walked up the road from the bus stop, to see that Acorn House was still standing.

She was even more relieved, as she mounted the second flight of stairs, to hear the sound of voices pitched at an ordinary conversational level, with no indication of trauma or crisis. She was actually glad to hear Alistair's annoying tones, mocking something someone had just said. Normally she would have been distinctly put out to discover Alistair already here before midday on a Saturday, as it would almost certainly mean that they would have him for the whole weekend. This time, though, after all her fears and imaginings, his familiar provoking presence was positively reassuring. So much so that she even found herself smiling when he stretched out his arms towards her in idle greeting and lamented the fact that he was too lazy to get off the sofa to come and kiss her.

"If a man be a fool" she quoted, "Pray God that he may also be lazy, for it will keep him out of many troubles," and soon she had joined them in what had obviously been something of a marathon coffee-break.

By now, Norah's former reticence was quite gone. She seemed only too glad to tell and re-tell her unhappy story. After all the long months of secrecy, of trying to hide her tragic family situation from friends and neighbours, of enduring the social isolation which inevitably goes with hiding one's real situation from absolutely everybody, she found it an indescribable relief to be confiding at last in listeners who were not only interested but, far more important, had never known her as the person she once was. Among strangers, there was hardly any pain involved in playing the role of victim, because they have never known any other way; to *become* a victim, a "Poor Thing", under the shocked gaze of old friends who had previously known you as an amusing, life-enhancing, top-of-the-world sort of person, was humiliating beyond all endurance.

So, having already told her story in such detail to Diana, Norah was now quite ready to repeat the salient points for Bridget's benefit.

"So you see, Bridget," she explained, "The reason I've run away like this isn't just that I can't stand it, though of course I can't. What I think I'm really trying to do is to force Mervyn to realise that Christopher is mentally ill, so that he will be *forced* to do something about it. Get him treated somehow – get him into hospital – *something*. I *know* that that's what he needs, and if Mervyn is left to cope with him single-handed for even a few days, then he'll find it out for himself. You see, all the time I'm there he can get away with turning a blind eye to the awful things Christopher does, because I'm the one coping with the results. You see, the point is, Mervyn finds it intolerably humiliating to face the fact that he, a top-ranking psychiatrist, has a mentally-ill son. But if I'm not there, he'll *have* to face it. When he comes home and finds that Christopher has wrecked something for some weird reason inside his head – and when he can't blame it on me, whatever it is, because I'm not there – then he'll *have* to face it, won't he? He'll *have* to do something about it."

"Such as what?" put in Alistair drily. "Haven't you heard of Community Care? Don't you know what it means? It means *you*. On the job 24 hours a day, seven days a week, without any pay at all – what could be cheaper? And in the case of *your* son – you won't even get anyone doing an assessment or prescribing the appropriate pills for him to refuse to take. Since the patient's father is some kind of a shrink, they'll assume that *he's* seeing to all that kind of thing, because he's the expert."

Here he sighed, and raised his eyes to the ceiling in mock despair.

"Nobody seems to understand what an expert is, and what can be expected of him. As an expert myself, in a small way, I can tell you. An expert is the man who can't be expected to *do* anything. He's there simply to criticise the people who *do* do things."

"But, Alistair, he'll *have* to do something! You don't understand!" Diana interrupted. "The kind of things this boy gets up to when he's in one of his bad spells – tell him, Norah. Tell him some of the things you've told me."

And Norah, willingly enough by now, did so.

"I'd let him go out shopping," she began. "I did that sometimes, when he seemed to be having a good day, and mostly he was very efficient. I was upstairs when he arrived back, and when I came down I found he'd brought home this load of groceries from the supermarket and had put it all in the washing-machine. With detergent, and switched on to "Hot". If I hadn't been there to cope with the worst of the mess before Mervyn got home – if he'd come in and found the butter and the Rainbow Dip and the soused herrings and bananas all whirling round, and no one but himself to do something about it . . . Mind you, he got involved in the end, because we had to get a man in to fix the washing machine. The works were all bunged up with gunge even after I'd cleaned it . . . Mervyn blamed *me*, of course. He said I didn't understand that someone as brilliant as Christopher was bound to be a bit absent-minded at times.

"But it wasn't absence of mind, I knew it wasn't, it was full-blown delusion. Christopher explained it to me in his weird, logical-sounding way. He was afraid of food-poisoning, he said, from the modern methods of chilling and storing, and so he'd decided that all super-market food should be given a thorough wash before being eaten.

"But Mervyn *still* managed to blame me. And that's why I think that without me there – with no one to blame but Christopher himself . . . Without me there, he'll *have* to . . ."

"Hasn't it occurred to you that he might walk out too? Just like you did? If *I* came home and found the washing machine churning up the muesli and the gorgonzola and the smoked salmon and the Mothers' Pride, I'd be through the front door before you could even turn it to 'Wool and Fine Fabrics' . . ."

At Alistair's throwaway contribution to the problem, Norah gave a little gasp of dismay.

"Oh *no*! Oh, surely he wouldn't! Oh, I never thought of that! When I rang Christopher last night, he never mentioned his father at all. I wonder if that might mean . . . Oh, my God! If he's been actually *alone* all this time . . .!"

She was actually biting her nails now, her restless brown eyes darting from one face to another; her whole body was tense and somehow shrunken, like a cornered mouse.

"Oh, he wouldn't!" she said again, in tones which made it perfectly clear that he *would*. Or might. Or already had. Who knew what a man would do when brought face to face with the unendurable?

"Oh, what shall I do? Oh, I should never have . . .! Oh, I must go back! I must see what's going on . . . I don't know *what* he might get up to, all on his own like that! And the neighbours . . .!"

It was impossible not to notice the eager, almost hungry look on Diana's face while this exchange was going on, and Bridget realised that the possibility of interviewing Norah for the forthcoming Community Care programme was taking shape in her friend's mind, in spite of her earlier protestations about it being unethical to interview friends.

Why should it be? What was wrong with it – if Norah was willing? Bridget recalled Diana's disappointment on learning that Norah was a dead loss for the Battered Wives programme – but was there not a future programme already in the pipe-line on the subject of Community Care? And Norah's predicament was not merely that of the run-of-the-mill carer of any mental patient. Hers displayed a new and intriguing angle: the problem of the carer whose partner refuses to recognise that there is a problem at all. Partnership difficulties were bound to be quite a feature of the new series, Bridget reflected. Diana had already mentioned cases in which marriages had broken up because one partner – usually the husband – simply could not stand the stress and the social stigma. But in Norah's situation there was this new and piquant twist of the husband refusing to recognise the truth. Norah had already shown herself willing to reveal all to three near-strangers; might she not be equally willing – even eager – to reveal her problems to millions of viewers? It was amazing how many people *were* willing to do just this. Why shouldn't Norah be one of them?

It would have to be done anonymously, of course. Bridget tried to visualise Norah in silhouette, with her back to the camera, and her voice scrambled into near-inaudibility.

Even so, Diana would have to go carefully, Bridget reflected. Her approach would have to be tentative, and very reassuring.

"I tell you what, Norah," Diana was saying, as if as a footnote to Bridget's speculations, "Why don't I drive you down there this afternoon? I can see you're anxious about how your son is managing; of course you are; but if you are planning to go and see for yourself, I think you ought to have someone with you. Someone to spy out the land, as it were. I mean, your husband may easily still be there, he might answer the door to you, and I gather that would be a bit of a disaster. So what I'm thinking of is this. If we went together, I could leave you in the car while I went ahead to your house and sussed it out. I could find out who's in and who isn't in, and roughly what's going on. If it's a boy who answers the door, and he seems to be alone in the house, then I'll signal to you to come along. If it's a middle-aged man, I'll think up some plausible pretext: Market Research, or canvassing for the Labour Party, or something."

"Jehovah's Witnesses would be best," contributed Alistair. "You'll look perfect for the part, sweetie, with that moist and soulful look you always have in your eyes when you are on the trail of your next T.V. victim. We'll borrow a Bible from the local vicar and confront Norah's hubby with a suitable text – 'He that diggeth a pit shall fall into it' – something like that. You'll be

87

an absolute wow, darling, I can just see you! When you tell him that the end of the world is nigh, he'll positively shake in his polished Consultant shoes. The only thing is, darling, I thought your ricketty little clapped-out banger was having its MOT test this afternoon. Doesn't that throw a spanner in the do-goodery? For today, anyway?"

"Yes . . . Well . . ." Diana hesitated. "They said it would be ready by three, and so I thought . . ."

"You thought it would be ready by three, is that what you're trying to tell me? You really make me wonder whose head it is that wants examining. There's no chance at all that you'll get to this God-forsaken place before night. Somewhere in Hertfordshire, didn't you say? Look, why don't *I* take you both? And Bridget too. I'll take you all out to lunch, if you think you can afford it. I've at least mastered the Women's Lib principles about lunching with a chauvinist pig, and I heartily approve of them. Especially when it's *three* of you."

And lurching from the sofa with surprising agility, he donned his anorak, located his car keys, and stood waiting, apparently taking for granted the acquiescence of all concerned.

Chapter 11

As they worked their way through the weekend traffic towards the M1, Bridget, sharing the back seat with Norah, was wondering what on earth had induced her to get involved in this hare-brained excursion. Partly, it was because she had nothing else to do. Having carefully and painstakingly organised herself a free weekend in which to pay a duty visit to her parents, she was now in the rare and delightful situation of having ahead of her a day and a half of totally uncommitted time. So rare and so unexpected was this situation that it had rather gone to her head, and put her in the mood to say "Yes" to things. Partly, too, she had been moved by Norah's earnest and anxious persuasion. It seemed that Norah was actually frightened of going back to her house alone. She wanted to gather around her a sort of body-guard against whatever might be in store. Nothing that Bridget had heard so far of the unfortunate woman's troubles had suggested that the schizophrenic son was given to violence. His behaviour as so far described seemed weird in the extreme, but in no way dangerous.

Was it her husband, then, that she feared? Not for the threat of actual physical violence – a man in his position, and with such exaggerated concern for his

status and reputation, would hardly risk the publicity of a summons for beating up his wife – but maybe his rages were in themselves terrifying; and rage undoubtedly could be expected by his runaway wife.

The third reason for her being in the back of the car – and this was one which Bridget did not enjoy admitting, even to herself – was sheer, vulgar curiosity. Something dramatic, exciting, was almost bound to happen, and she wanted to be in on it. Exactly like those crowds that gather so eagerly round a road accident. Surely she, Bridget Sadler, was above such crude impulses?

"What superior thoughts are you thinking right now, superior little one?" Alistair enquired suddenly, half-turning over his shoulder; "Why so quiet?" – but before she had time to answer, he had hastily turned his attention back to the road ahead, where an enormous lorry seemed about to move into his lane.

"Careful, darling!" Diana murmured nervously into his ear; and a moment later they all pitched forward in their seats as he braked violently.

"The damn swine – he's crossed on the yellow – *I'll* show him!" he swore, and for the next few minutes Bridget kept her eyes shut. He was an awful driver. She heard Diana's little gasps of dismay – not that it took much to make Diana gasp – and at one point the driver himself exclaimed "Oops!" and the car lurched this way and then that.

Presently, however, Alistair's speed steadied, and Bridget opened her eyes. The suburbs were thinning out now, the rows of houses giving way here and there to a tired field or two, or a building site. They were in Hertfordshire now. Almost in the country. Great trees lined the road, and beyond them could be glimpsed occasional pastures and herds of cows. Alistair looked about him with satisfaction.

"Nearing Loony Land, aren't we" he queried, tossing the remark backwards towards Norah, who cowered silently in the back seat. "Aren't there more loony bins to the square mile here than anywhere else in Europe?" Then, when Norah failed to respond, he continued: "This is your home ground, isn't it? I'm going to need your guidance. Where do I turn off?"

"Oh! I – well – that is . . ." Norah, who hitherto had scarcely spoken, looked almost as frightened as if it had been her husband himself suddenly addressing her. "I – well, you see, I don't drive . . . But I know the way from the station," she added placatingly. You could tell that she was a practised non-map-reader, who had evolved, more or less unconsciously, such skills as were necessary for getting out of the task. "I should think there'll be a signpost, won't there?" she suggested timidly, and then fell silent.

"Women!" snorted Alistair, and over his shoulder shoved a road map into Bridget's lap, as if she wasn't a woman herself.

Quickly, she found the relevant page, directed him to the right turn-off, along a country road with soaking grass verges and leafless hedgrows, into an area that Norah recognised, and finally into the actual road where she lived. As they slowed down, nearing No 20, Norah clutched Bridget's hand, and all the long unhappy years glittered in her eyes.

"No – Oh please! – Not quitc so near!" she begged "Can't you park a little way further on?" And Alistair, with an expressive shrug of his shoulders, by-passed number 20 and parked at the far end of the road.

91

"Now what?" he said; and they all looked at each other.

Bridget was determined not to be the one to make any suggestions. None of it was anything to do with her, and so she turned her face away and looked determinedly out of the window.

It wasn't a very attractive road, and on this damp autumn afternoon it was looking its least attractive. It was respectable enough – clipped hedges, neat front gardens, each with its square of wet lawn and its row of savagely-pruned roses. From well-weeded strips of dark earth rose clumps of unidentifiable dark foliage, perennials, presumably, from which, come summer, bright blossoms might emerge. The houses were bay-windowed, semi-detached, not at all handsome but neat and well-kept, with recently painted gates and front doors. Almost all the bay windows were shrouded by net curtains, giving the impression that all of them, not just Number 20, had some uneasy secret to keep.

"Well, here we are," Alistair pointed out again. "Come on, Norah, do your stuff. It's for you to allot the parts. Just remember, though, that I'm not going to do anything macho about these crazy men-folk of yours. Not my scene."

"Shall I go first, like we said?" Diana offered. "I might say I'm looking for a Mrs Wilson, and I'm afraid I might have got the wrong address. Something like that. So long as there isn't a real Mrs Wilson living nearby. I don't want to get caught up in . . ."

"No . . . no there isn't," quavered Norah "Not that I know of, anyway. Yes, do that, will you Diana? And if Christopher *is* on his own . . ."

"Then I'll wave," Diana assured her, and climbed out

92

of the car. They all watched as she set off down the road, her high-heeled boots clicking on the damp pavement, and her loose scarlet jacket swinging as she walked. She walked briskly, purposefully, as if she really had got important business to transact with this Mrs Wilson.

They watched her turn in at the gate of Number Twenty, traverse the short gravel path and raise her hand to the bell when she reached the front door.

There was a pause of several seconds; long enough, anyway, to be too much for Norah. She turned away from the window and so had no glimpse of the person who finally answered the door. Not that the others could see much, either; just a tallish figure largely obscured by the shrubs around the porch and by the door itself, which was only partially opened, as if by someone uneasy about who the caller might be.

For a few moments they watched Diana speaking – making polite little gestures; and then, after less than a minute, she disappeared into the house, the door closing behind her.

"Did she – did she wave to me?" Norah at last ventured to ask; and when Bridget shook her head, and described what they had managed to see, Norah gave a little squeal of dismay.

"Oh! Oh, then, it wasn't Christopher! It must have been Mervyn! Why hasn't she come straight back? What is she *doing*?"

What indeed? A preliminary softening-up session with the father in the case? Bridget refrained from frightening her tremulous companion with the suggestion that a TV interview might be on the cards; and, in any case, a few moments' reflection convinced her that the suspicion was unfounded. In the context of a programme aimed at wrenching heart-strings over intimate family problems, a father who insisted that there *wasn't* a problem would be a non-starter.

No point in guessing at this stage. Diana would explain it all when she came back.

But when *would* she come back? Already she had been gone for quite a long time – twenty minutes at least. Bridget consulted her watch; and presently, when a full hour had passed, and the winter daylight was already beginning to fade, she leaned forward and gave Alistair a sharp prod between the shoulder-blades.

"I think we ought to *do* something," she said to the large, slumped back in front of her, watching it stir reluctantly. Either he had been asleep or he had been pretending to be – a good ploy for anyone who wanted to avoid whatever is going to happen next.

"Good idea," he agreed. "Off you go. Don't worry about me, I'll be quite comfortable here on my own."

Before Bridget had thought up a sufficiently stinging rejoinder to his pusillanimous suggestion, she was interrupted by a little cry of relief from Norah and a spasm of her slight body as she jerked bolt upright.

"Diana! She's coming! Look, she's waving . . . Oh, thank goodness!" and through the gathering twilight they could see Diana hurrying – indeed running, as much as she could in those stylish boots – towards them.

"Oh, he's so handsome!" were her first words. "An absolute smasher! Photogenic to the N'th degree!"

Who was? Christopher, or the dreaded Mervyn? But Diana's next words set Norah's immediate fears to rest.

"Come on, Norah! He wants to see you, he really

does. I'm sorry I've been so long, but I had to make sure his father wasn't there. I mean, he might have been in the garden or somewhere. But he's not. Christopher isn't expecting him back till quite late, so now is your time. He's waiting for us."

Still Norah seemed to hesitate. Her first surge of relief at Diana's reappearance seemed to be fading, and once again she clutched at Bridget's hand.

"Please come with us," she begged. "I'm . . . That is, I wouldn't like . . . But with *three* of us . . . Of course I know he wouldn't hurt a fly, but . . ."

For the second time that afternoon Bridget found herself unsure of her true motivations. One of them, certainly, was to put Alistair to shame, there where he lounged, once again tactically asleep, behind the steering-wheel. How cowardly can you get? Not that accusations of cowardice would have succeeded in putting him to shame, not in the least. Alistair treasured his failings as if they were essential qualifications for the good life. Which perhaps they were? But by now the threesome were out in the street, hurrying to their destination, and Bridget had to abandon her self-searching.

Chapter 12

Handsome, Smashing. Photogenic. Meeting Christopher Payne for the first time, Bridget felt she could have endorsed all these epithets. He had a charming smile, too, and as he greeted her, so tall, so fair, and somehow aristocratic-looking, she found it almost impossible to believe that there was anything at all the matter with him. With a positively heart-warming display of old-world courtesy, he helped her off with her coat and led her into what was evidently the family sitting-room, and soon she was settled in one of the large, old-fashioned armchairs that filled a large proportion of the available floor-space. The whole room was, by Bridget's standards, sadly over-furnished. With its patterned curtains, patterned carpet and patterned upholstery, it had a restless air, and Bridget found herself wondering, idly, whether a small boy's psyche might actually have been affected by being brought up amid so many clashing patterns and decorations? A ridiculous idea really, and one that would never have occurred to her had she never been told that her young host was mentally unbalanced. Absurd to think that his parents' taste in furnishings could seriously upset a child's mental balance. All over the world children are brought up amid all sorts of surroundings. They are brought up in cardboard boxes, in royal palaces, in disused railway sidings, in high-rise flats, in mud huts, in isolated farmhouses, and there is not a shred of evidence that any one of these environments produces more – or fewer – schizophrenics than any of the others.

Really, she must stop thinking of this polite and well-mannered young man as a schizophrenic. Whether he was or wasn't, it was unfair to regard this as his defining quality, and to weigh up everything he did or said with reference to it.

"I expect you'd like some tea after your journey," he said, "I'll go and . . ."

But almost immediately the courteous gesture was quite spoiled – it seemed to Bridget – by Norah scrambling clumsily to her feet and interrupting him.

"No, no, Chris, dear, it's all right, I'll make it," she cried, and hastened, as if for dear life, out of the room and towards the kitchen.

This left Christopher alone with the two visitors. Unlike most teenage boys when confronted by their mother's friends, he showed no awkwardness or embarrassment, but made convincing small-talk until his mother returned, pushing a trolley of hastily-assembled tea-things. Then he helped gracefully with the passing-round of biscuits and tea-cups. Shortly afterwards he excused himself, explaining that he had homework to do.

The three women looked at each other. In the circumstances, it was difficult to know what to say.

"What a charming boy!" Bridget commented at last. This, surely, could do no harm, and was incidentally true.

Diana expressed whole-hearted agreement. "And not

only charming, but so self-possessed, and so easy to talk to. Such interesting ideas, too: you'd never guess that he was . . ." Here she stumbled to a halt, just in time, and hurried on, anxious to cover up her gaffe. "He and I had *such* an interesting talk before you came along. He told me all about his school, and what a pity it is they haven't got adequate science labs. He's hoping to go in for genetics, you know, and though they've got plenty of facilities for chemistry and physics, they can't apparently provide him with . . . What's the matter, Norah? Why are you looking like that?"

"Nothing. I'm not looking like anything," Norah mumbled; and then: "I'm just thinking, actually, that we ought to be going. I mean, we've left Alistair all on his own in the car . . . And now that I've seen that things here are going on all right – more or less – Yes, I think we should go."

Stepping out of the centrally-heated house into the outdoors was almost literally a breath-taking experience. The wind had risen since they were last outside and was hurling great blocks of jagged rain-cloud across the sky, bringing to the dull suburban street a sense of vast spaces, of unimaginable distance. The roadside trees were bending before it, creaking and swaying, and shadows from the bare twigs leaped and danced on the lamplit pavement.

The car was gone. At first, they thought that Alistair had simply grown fed up with waiting and had deserted them – no one would have put it past him – but a brief search revealed that this was not the case. He had simply driven round the corner into a road bordering the local park. Here the street lighting was sparse, the passers-by few, and he felt, he explained, less conspicuous.

"I was beginning to get funny looks, you see, parked there for hours and hours . . . ("Barely an hour!" Diana was protesting, but he silenced her with a look) For hours and hours outside Number 92. 'What gives at Number Ninety-two?' the passers-by must have been thinking, and the peerers from behind lace curtains; and it occurred to me that I might be in dead trouble if I stayed there. I mean, suppose some stupid kid gets herself murdered this very evening? All the neighbours will at once jam the police phones describing this disreputable and criminal-looking type they'd noticed lurking in a parked car all evening. Some of them will even have managed to recall the number. Amazing, isn't it, how people not only notice the number of other people's cars, but also remember it, days afterwards, when they are being interviewed. When did *you* last memorise the number of someone else's car? Still, that's how it is, and so that's why I moved on. I knew you'd find me in the end, especially with Cleversticks here (he jerked his elbow towards Bridget) to help you.

"So come on. Three chattering females on board will allay suspicion one hundred percent."

Diana slipped swiftly into the front passenger seat, while Norah wrestled ineptly with the rear door. Bridget seized a moment to look up at the black, star-spangled sky – the sort you never saw in London. Orion had risen, and Sirius; you could almost make out the seventh star of the Pleiades, so brilliant was the tangled web of them.

But now Alistair had switched on his headlights, and the heavens were obliterated.

The journey back, in the reverse direction to the rush-hour traffic, was comparatively speedy, and enlivened by Diana's enthusiastic – not to say ecstatic – account of her private conversation with Christopher.

"He was *wonderfully* forthcoming," she enthused. "He answered at length every single thing I asked him. I just love the way his yellow hair falls across his forehead when he tosses his head and smiles . . . it'll be brilliant on camera! He says he would *love* to be interviewed on television. He's into genetic engineering, you know – I think I told you. He's been working on spiders and on centipedes, and he'll soon be in a position to insert a gene for *intelligence* into them! Isn't that amazing? Genetic engineering is right at the top these days, after all that stuff about genes for homosexuality, and that mouse – the Onco-Mouse – with genetically-engineered cancer. It provoked more viewer-response even than sex-aids for the disabled. It'll be a winner! Jeremy'll get the production team onto it at once.

"The only thing is, though, Christopher thinks his father won't be too keen. He says his father's very rigid, and hide-bound by his professional status. So he suggests I come when his father's not there. Like tomorrow, he thought, as it's his father's weekend on duty . . ."

Here she paused, evidently choosing her words for the next bit.

"Of course, the whole thing will be completely anonymous, we don't need to involve Dr Payne at all; and I'm sure Norah won't object, will you, Norah? I mean, it'll be such a boost to the boy's self-confidence, won't it? Usually, no one listens to him, he says, and so to have *millions* of people, all listening . . ."

101

Here she turned right round in her seat to face Norah, the headlights of oncoming cars leaping in bars of light and shadow across her eager face.

"You wouldn't stand in his way, would you Norah? Surely you wouldn't?"

Chapter 13

Would she? Norah had evaded a clear answer as they raced along the motorway. What with the noise, and the speed, and the on-and-off darkness blurring the expression on one's face, it had been easy. But it was different once they were back at the flat, where Alistair had dropped them before speeding off to enjoy the rest of the weekend on his own – or not on his own, who could tell? Fortunately, Diana did not seem to be bothered. Not at the moment, anyway; she was far too busy telephoning people with names like Jeremy and Adrian about her exciting new project.

Lying on her bed, racked with nerves, Norah struggled to make out, through the half-open door, exactly what these telephone calls were about; but although she could hear clearly enough the high-pitched excited tones of the speaker's voice, the actual words were inaudible.

Was Diana, brazenly and selfishly, ignoring Norah's wishes in the matter? Or had she genuinely supposed that Norah's evasive murmur in the car had amounted to a tacit consent?

But what Diana might be thinking and believing was only half of the problem. The other half was Norah's own uncertainty and doubt. Because what Diana had

103

said was true – to be on television, expounding his bizarre views to millions, would indeed be an ego-boost to Christopher such as he hadn't enjoyed for years – not since he had been the mathematical boy-wonder enjoying the amazed adulation of parents and teachers and (to a lesser extent) the reluctant admiration of his class-mates.

Was an ego-boost exactly what he needed? Might it, conceivably, sweep the delusions once and for all from his contorted mind? Was he, perhaps, just on the point of recovery anyway? They do say, don't they, that no one ever does "recover" from schizophrenia – the most that can be hoped for is occasional remissions. On the other hand, there had never been any official diagnosis of schizophrenia in Christopher. On the contrary his father, an accredited expert on the subject had firmly and consistently denied that his son suffered from any mental illness at all.

Occasionally, over the dark and chequered years of Christopher's worsening spells of distorted thinking and bizarre behaviour, Norah had tormented herself with doubts about her own sanity. Could Mervyn possibly be right in his insistence that it was *her* neurotic and abnormal behaviour that compelled Christopher to behave neurotically and abnormally in self-defence? These thoughts would creep upon her whenever her son was in a "good" mood for any length of time – when he was enjoying a remission would be another way of putting it. During these spells he would be well-behaved, even good company, and would keep out of trouble at school. But each time, just as Norah was beginning to relax her guard; to hope, cautiously, that this might be the beginning of permanent recovery – at just this point, when her vigilance began to lapse – some new and awful thing would happen: an unpredictable and totally bizarre delusion would suddenly obsess him, and drive him to terrifying lengths of – well – of madness. No other word for it.

Like this genetic engineering fantasy, which had so intrigued Diana. Knowing nothing whatever about genetic engineering except that it achieved top ratings on T.V. programmes – and, terrifyingly, this was all that she needed to know – she seemed quite oblivious to the fact that everything Christopher had been telling her was complete and total nonsense. *Must* be nonsense. Even in the most advanced genetic-engineering centres in the world, they had only managed so far to engineer tiny modifications in existing creatures; and now here was an eighteen-year-old boy, still at school, and with no access to any sort of appropriate equipment – here was this boy assuring Diana that he, single-handedly, had engineered all sorts of new and extraordinary creatures; and that, yes, he could produce them in front of the cameras when required.

Rationally, one might assume that he was pulling her leg; but, alas, he wasn't. Norah was the only person in the world who could know for certain that he wasn't, because she was the one who had been there when it all began.

It had been a few months ago; and, as commonly happened, there had been a spell of comparatively quiet and acceptable behaviour before this latest leap into the darkness that lurked always, waiting, somewhere inside his skull.

It was a Wednesday afternoon, and Christopher for

some reason – maybe a quite legitimate one, she couldn't remember – was home from school. The two of them were in the sitting-room listening to a Mozart piano sonata on the radio. The piece had been a favourite of Christopher's – he had even played it when he was younger and when all his talents, musical and mathematical, were at their height.

The third movement was just coming to an end when, without warning, Christopher sprang from his deep armchair, hurled himself upon the set and slammed off the music in mid-bar.

"How dare they!" he muttered, "That's *my* frequency!" and he began, with urgent abandon, to switch from station to station, pausing nowhere. Broken sentences – half bars of music – snatches of foreign speech – unintelligible wails and bursts of laughter – a Shakespearian voice enunciating less than half a line from somewhere – at which, with an angry gesture, Christopher switched the thing off and turned on his mother.

"You heard that?" he challenged her. "All those channels – all those voices? All of them invisible, coming through the air – right? Yet everyone thinks *they're* real, don't they? Why are *mine* the only voices that no one believes are real? Listen . . ."

He sat absolutely still, his head tilted to one side, listening; and Norah found that she, too, was tilting her head on one side and listening. It seemed impossible not to do so. The intensity of a mad person's certainty is irresistibly compelling.

How long did they sit like this? She heard a car passing and then another. She heard a garden gate squeak, she heard footsteps on the pavement. After

106

a bit, she began to hear her own breathing, and then her own heart, thump, thump, thumping.

Presently, her son spoke.

"There! Didn't I tell you? Now you've heard it for yourself! They've given me the code – the genetic code! I must write it down immediately, I mustn't forget a single thing . . ." and he rushed upstairs.

Later, on his desk – that desk which she and Mervyn had bought with such pride for their brilliant son, all those years ago – she found, as she'd feared she would, the "genetic code". Pages and pages of cramped, tiny writing, dotted all over with tiny chemical formulae; illegible, unintelligible, and full of menace.

He was off again.

That evening he brought his mother a dead spider, its eight lifeless legs curled tightly around its belly. He explained to her that it had unfortunately died during the experiment in genetic engineering. "At first I thought I'd got one of the formulae wrong; but I've checked it right through, and everything's correct. The only other possibility is that it's the wrong kind of spider. I just found it, you see, in a corner of the ceiling, and that's much too random a way of locating specimens. You don't know what you're getting. In future, I'm going to make my own spiders, I shall genetically engineer them to be exactly as I want them. Then I *can't* go wrong. The next one will survive, I promise you."

And sure enough it did. It scuttled away at high speed the moment he laid it before her, and he crowed with delight.

"You see! It's worked! It's alive – I've given it life! It's *running*! Its legs are working, all eight of them – see?"

And Norah, coward that she was, had said Yes, she did see, and never argued at all. Well, what was the point? It would only cause a lot of upset, especially if Mervyn came to hear of it. And spiders, after all, were only spiders.

But Christopher's delusion didn't stop at spiders, or even at centipedes. In her heart, Norah had known it wouldn't. She wasn't prepared, though, for the genetically-engineered mouse, four times the size of a normal mouse, that turned up in her kitchen a few days later. Cowardly as she had now become, she congratulated Christopher on this remarkable success, and then, later, while he was at school, she bribed the rat into a corner with a piece of bacon, and then, protected by a stout pair of gardening gloves, she captured the creature and dropped it over the fence at the bottom of the garden onto a patch of waste land.

"I'm so sorry, it seems to have run away," she'd planned to lie to her son; but by the time he got home he had lost interest in the creature.

"I'm into something much, much bigger!" he assured her, with a sinister note of glee in his voice, and went off upstairs "to prepare the blue-print" for his next venture. Pages and pages of it, including diagrams of weird and intricate machines, One of these, it turned out, was a machine designed for sewing free-range eggs together – a necessary preliminary, apparently, to the achieving of the Grand Design.

All too soon, the nature of the Grand Design was revealed to her: nothing less than the genetic engineering of a complete human being. This, he explained to her, his blue eyes shining like warning lights with a terrifying triumph, had been his target all along.

"You always have to start with animals for this kind of research," he solemnly explained, and went off upstairs to put the final touches to the blue-print for the perfect human being.

Had he actually been telling Diana all this? Had he showed her those pages of gobbledygook, and had she really been convinced by it? Though actually all she needed to be convinced about was that the cramped lines of handwriting and the weirdly complex diagrams would come out well on the TV screen. Probably they would. After all, no one was going to try and read them; they'd be flashed on and off the screen far too quickly. They did this routinely in serious science programmes, so why not?

What else had he and Diana talked about? Norah had been relieved, of course, to find Christopher in one of his "good" moods on the afternoon of their arrival. He tended to be at his best, at his apparently sanest, when in the company of strangers. She recalled, now, that disastrous party to which he had invited half the neighbourhood without warning. She remembered his pleasant smile, his courteous bearing towards the guests as they converged, bewildered, on the unsuspecting household.

That was just the way he'd behaved this afternoon. Norah had been thankful – naturally she had – that her son was presenting such an acceptable image to the visitors. The hideous embarrassments she'd dreaded simply had not occurred. Why, she might even have risked letting him make the tea. At the time, she had dreaded that he might add to the tea-bags some incongruous substance that suddenly caught his fancy; but she realised now that this probably wouldn't have

109

happened, so "good" was the mood he was in. His behaviour throughout the visit had been impeccable. No one would have guessed that there was something terribly wrong with him.

There were moments when she couldn't even believe it herself. Was she (as Mervyn kept assuring her) imagining things? Once again, she found herself in the grip of those doubts about her own sanity which are an occupational hazard for carers in her situation. To be in the presence of distorted thinking twenty-four hours a day, seven days a week, takes its toll in the end. One picks up the distorted logic in just the same way as one picks up a foreign language when living abroad; it lodges in the brain effortlessly, and almost without conscious awareness.

Was this what was happening to her? Was she gradually turning into a person to whom this could happen? What sort of person *was* she turning into, under the worsening stresses of her life?

In a moment of near-panic, she scrambled off the bed, switched on the top light as well as the bedside lamp and headed for the wardrobe, which had a full-length mirror on the inside of the door.

It was difficult to get the illumination quite right. She set the door open at this angle and at that angle: she moved the bedside light from here to there and back again, until at last adequate illumination fell upon her ravaged face.

Yes, ravaged. That was the only word for it if you looked closely, really closely, as she was looking now, peering intently at every single line, following its course across the puckered brow, and from the base of the nose to the corners of the tightly-compressed mouth.

No one – absolutely no one, looking at her now – would guess that Norah was only a little over forty. She could easily be sixty. And worse than that – far worse – she wasn't *herself* any more. She could still remember herself quite well – a happy, outgoing young girl who went in for tap-dancing. A girl with bright eyes and a ready smile, making new friends wherever she went. Even Mervyn had been proud of her in those days; he'd loved to take her to the various social functions at the hospital, and she had been able to hear the pride in his voice when he introduced her to colleagues as his wife. "This is my wife, Norah . . ." She was an asset to him in those days. He loved her.

This shouldn't have happened to me, she raged silently, staring into the worn and defeated face. I wasn't the right kind of person to be struck by tragedy. I was a cheerful, carefree sort of person, who should have had a cheerful, carefree sort of life. A person enjoying her daily round, and enhancing the enjoyment of those around her by her light-hearted gaiety. That was the person I was meant to be, that was my inborn nature. That was *myself*. This person; this one in the mirror, shattered and dulled by the tragedy of having a schizophrenic son, – it just isn't *me*. It can't be.

It is, though. This is how it happens. This light-hearted person who is simply not suited to tragedy -- when tragedy *does* strike, it changes her, slowly and inexorably, into a person who *is* suited to tragedy. It may take months, it may take years, but it will happen.

It *has* happened. To *me*.

With a surge of revulsion, Norah slammed the wardrobe door shut, blotted out the unnatural creature in the mirror and flung her selfback onto the bed to sob the night away.

Or some of it, anyway. One always goes to sleep in the end. This, at least, was one thing she had learned.

Chapter 14

Bridget heard the wardrobe door slam shut. Indeed, it had shaken the whole flat, as well as the table on which she was working, but it had not occurred to her to go and find out if anything was wrong. She was busy, making notes on an article on the Polish gas industry which she was going to have to translate from the French tomorrow. She needed to be familiar with the relevant technical terms in both languages before going into the Conference hall tomorrow, and so the banging of the door was no more than an annoying interruption.

It *was* annoying, though; and it *had* interrupted her. It had made her feel irritable, all over again, about this tiresome new flatmate of theirs. Her original objections to giving house-room to this unhappy lady had been, she felt, amply vindicated. Further and further complications seemed to be accumulating round the bothersome little creature, and this was affecting everyone. Already, Bridget and Diana had been lured into spending an entire Saturday afternoon on Norah's problems. Well, no, that wasn't quite fair. It hadn't been Norah's urging that had made them accompany her on the expedition, it was Diana who had been so keen – not to say hell-bent – on exploiting Norah's traumatic situation for the "Heart to Heart" programmes.

There was nothing wrong with that, in itself. It was her job, after all, to track down photogenic disasters, especially in family situations. "Exploiting" wasn't quite fair either, because Norah had seemed greatly relieved at the prospect of having company on a distinctly frightening expedition. After all, the oppressive husband *might* have been there, and it had been Diana who had undertaken, quite inventively, to eliminate that risk.

But now, it seemed, a repeat performance was planned for tomorrow. They would be driving down there again, this time in Diana's car, and Diana would once again be interviewing the crazy boy presumably in greater detail this time, and with a heavy slant towards action-bites. "We want to avoid talking heads as much as we possibly can," she'd explained recently, and so she would be setting Christopher up to do – well, what? What *did* you get a schizophrenic to do which would illustrate his schizophrenia to a sufficiently titillating degree, without offending against the increasingly complex and panicky rules about invasion of privacy which, according to Diana, were proliferating in her trade to a frustrating degree.

And how – why – had Bridget allowed herself to be drawn into this second adventure? This was the really annoying thing, and it was this, really, that had made that slamming door as annoying as it was.

The worst part of it was that Bridget had only herself to blame. She could have said "No". Even more galling was the fact that her Sunday was still empty of engagements. So there was no way she could say, "Sorry, I've got to do so-and-so". Everyone knew that the cancelled visit to her parents had left her day totally and uncharacteristically free.

So she had said "Yes" when she ought to have said "No". Actually, Diana had been very pressing: she was nervous about the trip, that was obvious. Twice she had asked Norah, in a studiedly offhand manner, whether there was any risk of Christopher turning violent. She had clearly been rendered uneasy by Norah's slightly evasive assurances. So she welcomed the idea of an extended body-guard on the premises. Diana was good at her job, with a knack for establishing an intimate rapport with her subjects; but even for her the initial approach must sometimes present difficulties. Sheer brazen cheek was sometimes required to initiate these exchanges; to surmount that fraught moment of getting across to a total stranger the idea that their personal disaster was going to be fun to watch. Not in those words, of course; and, as Diana often pointed out, some victims liked it. Some found that it lifted them up and out of their miseries like a powerful euphoric drug.

But some didn't. And if it turned out tomorrow that Christopher was one of these, what might he not do, unbalanced as he was. The fact that yesterday he'd liked the idea of being on television was no guarantee that he'd like it again tomorrow.

Bridget could have kicked herself for being so feeble, for letting herself get involved. But she secretly knew that she'd have kicked herself even harder if she'd kept aloof from it all, and had missed out on the whole adventure.

Chapter 15

The drive down to Medfield, with Diana at the wheel, was a good deal pleasanter than the previous day's. The weather was pleasanter, too. The wind had dropped, the rain-clouds had been blown away, leaving one of those winter skies of magical blueness, out of which the low sun sent a slanting light across the stubble fields and newly-ploughed furrows. They were passing now through that meagre stretch of real country that lay between London and their destination, and Bridget found herself able to enjoy the scene, in a mild way, now that it was not overlaid by the tensions inseparable from Alistair's show-off driving style. Perhaps the whole afternoon was going to prove mildly enjoyable after all? She was beginning to be quite glad she had come.

Norah had a key, of course, so when Christopher did not answer her ring on the bell, she opened the door and ushered her companions into the hall. The fact that he hadn't answered the bell was beginning to twang at her nerves, already taut with apprehension. What was he doing? Was he so obsessively absorbed in something that he hadn't heard the bell? Or had he chosen not to answer it?

Tremulously, from the foot of the stairs, Norah called her son's name. "Christopher!" she quavered, almost *sotto voce*, as if she didn't really want him to hear her; and then, visibly pulling herself together, she called again, a lot louder, her voice almost a scream: "Christopher! Where are you? We're here! Come on down!" and already, as the echoes rose and died away round the bend of the stairs, she knew he wasn't there. The others knew it too. There is something unmistakable about an absence. Everyone is aware of it, always.

This did not, of course, prevent them (it never does) from thoroughly exploring the place, opening every door. They even tried the door of Mervyn's study, but of course it was locked, as it always was when he was not there.

Back in the entrance hall, the three looked at each other.

"It's not that we're too early," Diana volunteered, looking at her watch. "Three o'clock was the time he specially asked me to come, and it's a quarter past already."

She, and Bridget likewise, now looked at Norah. The next move was up to her. This was her home. Her son.

"He – he must have gone out," she murmured – a remark so obvious, so inane, that she was not surprised that it drew upon her one of Bridget's impatient put-downs. "Really? And what else can we deduce from the fact that he's not in?" she enquired drily; but added, almost immediately, and remorsefully: "I'm sorry, Norah, I do see that you must be worried . . ."

Worried, yes indeed. Though of course Bridget couldn't have known about the thoughts that were darting like silver-fish through Norah's over-active mind: "He's *out*! He's out *by himself*! What is he up to? Is he upsetting the neighbours? What have his voices told him to do – and to whom?" Or had he, perhaps – and despite her fears, this quite commonly happened – had he gone off on some perfectly sensible errand? Shopping, perhaps? or to call on a friend?

Except, of course, that he hadn't any friends. An acquaintance, then? He might, just possibly, be next door at Louise's. Once, long ago, it had been almost a second home to him, when he and Louise's Peter, as small boys, had been in and out of each other's houses quite a lot. Was it possible that, magically, this old closeness had somehow been revived? It was a wild hypothesis, considering the rift which had developed between the two families in recent years. Still, there could be no harm in asking. She and Louise were still on speaking terms, though the old intimacy had long cooled into mere politeness. However, on this occasion mere politeness would be enough. "Yes" or "No" would be all that Louise needed to say.

"I think I'll just pop in next door," she explained to her companions, "They may know . . ." and before she had decided how to finish the sentence she was out through the front door.

Louise was surprised to see her, naturally – well, they'd hardly spoken for weeks. She even seemed cautiously pleased. When all else has failed in a relationship, curiosity can still keep it going after a fashion, and Louise was clearly curious to know what had been happening to her neighbour all this time; in particular, she was curious to hear the reason for Norah's recent

119

disappearance. Had her marriage finally broken up, like so many in the street?

But Norah, anxious and in a hurry, was not very forthcoming: which was a pity, because this was a moment when the old friendship might have been restored. She refused Louise's invitation to come in for a cup of tea, and instead stood hovering on the doorstep, radiating unease. She'd only dropped in for a moment, she explained, to ask if Louise had any idea where Christopher might be this afternoon?

But Louise, disappointed at this rebuff to her tentative overtures, knew nothing.

"We haven't seen anything of any of you, for weeks," she pointed out, not unreasonably. "No, I haven't the faintest idea what Christopher is doing. How would I? He never comes in here any more. He and Peter don't hit it off any more, do they?" Distant. Aggrieved. The moment for rapprochement was over, and Norah retreated, apologising as she went.

Her companions had by now succeeded in making themselves cups of tea in the unfamiliar kitchen, and were now seated in the sitting-room, heads together, talking. About *her*, Norah found herself instantly suspecting; but instantly rejected the thought. It wouldn't do for *her* to become paranoic as well, now would it?

Four o'clock now. A full hour after the appointed time, and still no Christopher.

"Well, I suppose we might as well be going," Diana was beginning, her usually up-beat tone flat with disappointment. "I do think though, after coming all this way . . ."

What she had thought was never to be revealed, for at that moment the front door opened. They all heard it:

120

they all felt the quiver of outside air passing through the house before the door was slammed shut and footsteps sounded in the hall.

"Christopher!" Diana exclaimed. "He's back!" She sounded alert, relieved, once more on the job.

But it wasn't Christopher. The tall and strikingly handsome man who now strode confidently into his own sitting-room was middle-aged and with greying hair still thick and abundant. His clean-cut features were not only outstandingly regular, they betokened a firmness of purpose, an unassailable self-confidence, that were somewhat intimidating to – outsiders, that is, reflected Bridget. To his patients, with their tremulous, mismanaged egos, he might well have come across as a tower of strength, a bulwark against unmanageable fear. His likeness to his son was minimal, Bridget noted, during those moments of embarrassed silence which succeeded his unexpected entrance. His complexion was dark where Christopher's was fair, his build sturdy and muscular where Christopher was slender and willowy. All the same, there *was* a likeness: something indefinable about the eyes. Although the father's eyes were grey and those of the son a clear and lucent blue, they both gleamed with the same sharp and wary intelligence. Yes, intelligence: however distorted it might be in the boy, it was still there behind the scenes, inextinguishable.

The silence stretched intolerably as the seconds mounted. Dr Payne was the first to speak.

"Well, my dear," he said, addressing his wife, "So you have decided to return home. How very sensible! Aren't you going to introduce your friends to me . . .?" – and then, when his wife remained paralysed

– by shock? – alarm? – embarrassment? – guilt? – whatever it was – he gave an apologetic little bow first to Diana and then to Bridget as they introduced themselves. Then Mervyn turned back, with a sort of controlled menace, towards his wife. Well, of course he was angry with her. What husband wouldn't be?

"Is this just a visit, my dear?" he asked her drily, "Or are you thinking of taking up residence here once more? It's entirely up to you. I'm not pressing you, I'm not even advising you. As you know, I never give advice to my patients, that's not my role. I just listen. So here I am, my dear. I am ready to listen. What have you to say?"

As he spoke he slowly, and somehow threateningly, lowered himself into one of the over-large, over-stuffed chairs. Once there, he placed the tips of his fingers together, and over this little parapet of knuckles and carefully-manicured nails, he watched his wife's face. Was this his usual pose when treating a patient, Bridget wondered? And did it, in their case, encourage them to talk? Or did it, as in Norah's case, make their faces twitch and grimace, and their words choke in their throats?

"Well, my dear," he prompted, after nearly a minute. "I'm waiting to hear what you have to say. You have been away now for the best part of a fortnight, putting your family to great inconvenience, and indeed to some anxiety. Out of consideration for your state of mind, I have so far refrained from contacting the police; although your behaviour has been such as to arouse legitimate concern for your safety. Wouldn't you agree?"

122

Norah by now seemed to have recovered the power of speech.

"I'm sorry," was all she could think of at first; and then, as her husband's enquiring gaze did not flicker, she went on: "I'm sorry, Mervyn, but I couldn't bear it any more."

"You couldn't bear it any more," he repeated consideringly – and Bridget remembered having read somewhere that this was part of the psychiatric technique – to repeat what the patient has just said. And indeed it seemed to work: "You couldn't bear it any more?"

"No, I couldn't!" Norah was speaking confidently now. "It's Christopher, Mervyn! You know it is! The awful things he keeps doing. And he's getting worse. I just can't cope . . ."

"You just can't cope," Mervyn repeated, but the technique didn't work this time. Sometimes it doesn't. And so after a few seconds he was forced to go on: "What is it that you can't cope with?"

Here he turned apologetically to the two visitors: "I'm sorry to be letting you in for this purely domestic discussion, but as you see, there is an important issue that has to be resolved between me and my wife. I hope you will forgive us." Then, focussing once again upon Norah, he asked "*What* is it you can't cope with?"

"I've told you! It's Christopher! All these mad delusions and obsessions! Dead spiders in the fridge! Sewing free-range eggs together with a darning needle! That sort of thing. I can't bear it. No one could bear it. Where is it going to end? Where is he right now? – He's up to something awful, I know he is . . ."

She paused, and for a moment buried her face in her hands. Then, looking up once more: "Oh, Mervyn, where *is* he? Is he *all right*? We've been her since three o'clock and there's been no sign of him. Where *is* he?"

It seemed to Bridget that the expression on Dr Payne's face resembled nothing so much as that of a committed bridge-player who finds himself with such a hand of winning cards as exceeds all the laws of probability. He turned to the two visitors with an air of almost uncontrollable triumph.

"You see?" he exclaimed. "You see what's going on in this family! A lad of *eighteen*, for God's sake, and he can't leave the house for as much as a couple of hours without his mother going into hysterics! This is mother-love gone mad! This is *smother*-love . . ." Then, turning to his wife:

"Well, never mind. Let's leave it for now. We mustn't inflict this sort of thing on our visitors. We've been through it all before, anyway, many, many times."

He waited a moment; but when his wife said nothing, he continued; "Listen, my dear, you still haven't answered my question: What have you come home *for*? And how long are you planning to stay? It would be convenient if I knew something of your plans."

"I *haven't* any plans. I *don't know* what I'm going to do. I've come back this weekend just to see if Christopher's all right . . . I mean, without me here . . ."

Dr Payne smiled; and this time the cat with the cream would perhaps be a more apt simile.

"My dear Norah! '*All right*', without you here! That's the under-statement of the year. Of course he's all right without you. He's more than all right. When you're not here he gets a chance to be his real self – all

124

those quirks of behaviour, which you provoke, they completely disappear, and he behaves exactly like any other normal boy of his age. He comes and goes on his own. He goes about with his friends. I suppose I'd better tell you, since you're interested, that he set off this morning on a camping trip with a couple of pals . . ."

"Where to? Which pals?" The words exploded from Norah's lips uncontrollably, though she must have known what their effect would be.

"See what I mean?" her husband remarked drily, addressing himself to the visitors "A lad of eighteen, going off on a camping trip with friends, and his mother goes into paroxysms of alarm about him! What sort of a life is that for a boy on the verge of manhood? Hard though I know it must be for you, Norah dear, you really have to face the fact that . . . Oh, by the way, he left a note for you. Did you find it? I think I saw it on the hall table, but maybe . . . Excuse me . . ." He was out of the room and back again in seconds with a closely-written sheet of foolscap. Hand-written, the writing so small and so cramped as to be quite difficult to read.

Norah took the note with shaking hands, and peered at it, bewildered. Then, setting it aside for a moment, she scrabbled briefly in her handbag.

"Oh dear!" she exclaimed, "My reading glasses!" she delved again in the bag, and continued: "I wonder if I left them in the car? You remember, Diana, I was looking at the map for you just after we turned off the motorway. And we left the car right at the top of the road, didn't we . . . Oh dear . . ."

She was scared, Bridget could tell, of walking alone

125

up the dark road to the corner by the park; and though, in general, Bridget despised such timidity, she felt pity as much as scorn for Norah. The poor woman was having a dreadful time, no doubt about it.

"Don't worry, Norah, I'll get them for you," she volunteered. I know just where they are, I saw them on the front ledge. Let's have the keys, Diana; I shan't be two minutes."

More like five, probably, but never mind. Clutching the car keys in her left hand, Bridget hurried through the lighted hall and out into the dark.

Chapter 16

Night had long fallen, and with eyes not yet dark-adapted after leaving the house, Bridget picked her way cautiously down the front garden path, bordered by wet, overgrown foliage. Only when she reached the gate did she notice a tall, silent figure standing under the adjacent street-lamp. The pale hair shone like gold under the lamplight, and the slender, gracefully-poised figure was so still that it could have been the statue of some long-dead mythical hero.

For a moment Bridget stood collecting her thoughts. Then:

"Good evening, Christopher," she said brightly, recovering from her first tiny moment of shock. When he still did not speak or move, she went on: "Are you just coming in, then?" He shook his head, and smiled. Was this the smile that Norah had once described as his "queer, unreal smile", the prelude to some fresh bout of bizarre behaviour?

"No, I'm not coming in, not yet," he answered her. "Actually, I was waiting for you to come out. I knew you would, at just this time."

"How do you mean, you knew I would? How could you? I only knew it myself a minute ago . . ."

"Of course you only knew it a minute ago. I was the

one who knew it all along. I programmed you to do it. You see, you are one of my creatures, I genetically engineered you. You can only do the things that I've programmed you to do, and I programmed you to come out of the house at just this time. And you *did* come out of the house. You see? It works! You have to do whatever I programme you to do."

To her secret shame, Bridget felt a quiver of alarm. She hastily crushed it. He was only a poor loony.

Still, she didn't believe in humouring people, not even poor loonies.

"Don't talk nonsense," she retorted sturdily. "And now, if you'll excuse me . . ." She turned away, and set off briskly in the direction of their parked car, only to be brought to a halt by a mocking chuckle just behind her.

"You see? I've programmed you to walk up the road towards the park, and so that's what you have to do. You have no choice."

"I *have* bloody got a choice! Up the road towards the park is where I happen to want to go," Bridget snapped, and set off again at a brisk pace – indeed, almost a run.

With his long, light strides he kept up with her easily, laughing softly as he kept alongside.

"Would you like me to tell you what I've programmed you to do at the top of the road?" he enquired pleasantly. "You are going to come to a standstill at a certain parked car, a Ford Escort, Registration number G 566 XPA. You are going to insert a key in the driver's door . . ."

"Of course I am. It's my friend's car, and she's asked me to get something out of it."

128

How does he know the make and number of our car, thought Bridget. He must have been lurking around when we arrived. Not that it matters. No sense in asking questions and thus prolonging his irksome presence.

She edged away from him, stepping from the pavement onto the road and quickening her pace. "And now, please, will you leave me alone? I'm in a hurry, I want to get back quickly."

"Of course you do. I made you that way. Here – listen –" and taking a strong grip on her shoulder he pulled her to a standstill. "Listen. I made you. You didn't exist until I genetically engineered you, complete with all your memories. I am the world expert in the genetic engineering of human beings. While the scientific pundits with their government research grants have been messing about with cancer cells and onco-mice and such trivia, *I* have been researching the genetic engineering of human beings. I started with centipedes, but of course they had too many legs, so I turned to spiders. I reduced the number of legs until there were only two; and then – and then, after a prolonged period of trial and error, I perfected the method. A secret method of my own. It involves the manipulation of hitherto unknown growth enzymes . . . Oh, it's too complicated to explain to you. I didn't engineer you a brain that could grasp this kind of thing. I didn't need to. You don't need much of a brain at all really, since the only movements you can ever make, the only thoughts you can ever think, are the ones I've built into you. Here –"

By now they had reached the car, and he gave a thin little squeal of triumph. "There! Didn't I tell you? A Ford Escort, just as I said! And now I'm going to make you

129

unlock it; I am going to make you lean inside . . . Yes, yes, you have picked up a spectacle case from the front ledge, that's exactly what I programmed you to do! And now – you are programmed to start walking again. Back down the road the way you came. It's all fixed for you – you can't do anything else!"

Can't I indeed! She looked at the opposite direction, across the intersecting road, beyond which lay the park with its shadowy trees and bushes looming darkly behind faintly gleaming railings. Suppose, just for the hell of it, she was to put paid to all his nonsense by walking in this direction instead of down the road?

What on earth would be the point? You couldn't reason with a person whose reasoning faculties are so grossly impaired. Besides, she was in a hurry to get back. But no sooner had she taken a single step in the "programmed" direction than a mad, triumphant chortle from her companion roused in her such a surge of defiance as overwhelmed common-sense, and almost before she knew it, her body had swung round on its heel and raced across the road ahead, taking her with it.

Once in the park, picking her way through the tangled darkness, with black masses of looming vegetation shaking drops of water over her at every step, Bridget realised how silly she had been. And what a waste of time the whole thing had been, too – hadn't she assured her friends that she'd only be a couple of minutes? Swiftly, she turned to retrace her steps; and even as she did so, she heard the squeak of the park gate.

Was it Christopher? Or some stranger? Whichever it was, she was determined not to be frightened – she, who so despised women who were scared to go out and

130

about by themselves after dark. But she knew that if you want to hang onto the luxury of despising other people for this sort of thing, you have to be very sure of your own credentials.

Bridget was very sure. She had long ago learned (in the primary school playground, as a matter of fact) that there were three ways of overcoming fear. First, you straightened your shoulders like a soldier on parade, and took two deep breaths. Second, you walked *towards* whatever seems to be menacing you – never away: and, third, whatever it was, whoever it was, you took the initiative. It was essential to speak first; make the first move.

All of which she did on this occasion.

"Good evening," she said to the dim oval of a human face which she could now just distinguish, like a great white fruit hanging from the dark branches to her left. At her words, the dim face seemed to attach itself to a tall dim body emerging from the bushes and blocking the path ahead.

Christopher, of course, still following her, still checking on her every movement in order to dove-tail it into his fantasy.

"This is where you will learn a lesson," he said. "This is where my early experiments in human engineering have to live because they are imperfect, and very, very dangerous. They have to keep out of sight. They are going to hate you because you are a perfect specimen and they are not. The one who hates you most is the one whose brain somehow got tangled in the mechanism and came out all wrong. He hates you, hates you, hates you, because *your* brain has come out right. By that time, I'd identified the fault, but too late to help him. He resents

131

it all the more because, physically, he is so perfect. He is tall, and slim, and strong, and a lock of his yellow hair falls across his forehead as he moves. He has beautiful blue eyes, too. The eyes are the windows of the soul. One day, he let me look through those windows – only in the mirror, of course, he was afraid to let me come any nearer. I looked through these blue windows, right through to the distorted brain behind them. I saw it, just that once, in all its horror, and I've never looked again. He is somewhere here, right now, among the bushes; I know it, I can feel it. You are going to meet him any minute now, and when you do, you must run, and run, and run."

For a moment, the pale face came within inches of her own, it streamed and glittered with the sweat of some violent emotion, and the lock of hair fell damply across the forehead.

"You must run, and run, and run!" – and with a thin, high-pitched laugh, the figure whirled around and disappeared round the bend of the path. Once again, she heard the clicking of the iron gate.

Only a few yards to go, really, but it seemed like a long, long walk. Never since early childhood had Bridget experienced this sensation of not daring to run because the very act of running can turn manageable fear into unmanageable panic. Not until she reached the car did the the thudding of her heart slow down and her breathing return to normal.

Christopher was there, waiting for her, and as she approached he gave another of his high-pitched laughs.

"You see? You see? I can make you do things! And now – watch – I'm going to make you walk down the road, back to the house."

This time, she wasn't going to argue. She had wasted too much time already. It was a nuisance, a humiliating nuisance, that her knees were trembling so that she could hardly walk, but she set off all the same in her chosen direction.

He was delighted. His little cry of triumph quivered in the air of the quiet, deserted street.

"You see? You see?" he kept repeating, as he paced alongside in his soft shoes. "You *are* walking back along the road! You have to do everything that I make you do. Soon, I am going to make you commit a murder. Yes, murder. One day, very very soon, you will be covered with blood – your hands, your face, your clothes – everything – and you will realise then that what I've told you is true. On that day, the truth will be staring you in the face; on that day, you will wish that you had believed me; but it will be too late . . . You will be in my power. I am the King of the World."

His long strides were keeping up with hers as she walked faster, and yet faster, finally breaking into a run.

"I've programmed you to run, and run, and run!" he almost shrieked as their two shadows leaped in unison from street-lamp to street-lamp along the empty pavement.

"In a minute," he cried, "I shall make you wrench open our garden gate, I shall make you race up our garden path, and I shall make you hammer, hammer, on the door, hoping they will let you in!"

Chapter 17

"Whatever happened to you? Is the car all right?"
Diana asked anxiously; and Bridget, having reassured
her on this point, and apologising vaguely for having
been so long, subsided into one of the big chairs to
consider what, if anything, to reveal about her recent
adventures. It seemed wiser, just for the moment, to
keep quiet about it. It could only trigger off another
spasm of Norah's maternal anxieties, and might well be
disastrous if Mervyn were to come back in the middle
of it, as he well might do. Besides, she needed time
to concoct a slightly modified version of events which
would not reveal her own panic. For she was the strong
one, was she not? She was the no-nonsense one who
would never panic about anything, and she preferred
it to stay that way.

Meanwhile Norah, re-united with her reading-glasses,
was peering anxiously at the script before her, bringing
it first close up to her face, and then an arm's
length away.

"It's terribly small – the writing," she complained. I
know Christopher does write a very cramped hand . . .
but not as small as this. I've always been able to read
it before."

She moved, so that the standard lamp shone straight

135

down on the document, and peered even closer.

"It's . . . I don't know . . . It's somehow . . . I can only read bits of it. 'Dear Mum,' he starts. But he doesn't call me 'Mum', not unless . . . That is, normally he calls me Norah. He says he 'Hopes I won't be worried' – I don't know why he should say that, because I *never* let him know that I worry, Never."

She went on reading: "We'll be pitching our tent in a grassy meadow near the farm buildings . . . Wonderful views towards the hills . . ."

Norah glanced up, bewildered. "Christopher doesn't *say* things like this. He doesn't look at views, he never has. He lives inside himself, not among views. And he'd never say "grassy meadow", The most he'd ever say would be "field".

She studied the document yet more closely:

"And the writing! It's small and cramped all right, but it's not *his*. I'm certain it isn't . . ."

Had Mervyn been listening outside the door? Or had he come in by chance just in time to hear his wife's suspicions? Or had he, indeed, not taken in any of it? His manner, polite and imperturbable, revealed nothing.

"Well, my dear, are you satisfied?" he enquired, walking across to his wife and holding out his hand for the paper. "Or does the fact that your son is actually *enjoying* himself, without you in attendance, throw you into one of your maternal panics? I must say you're looking rather pale – I wonder if there is anything more I can do to reassure you? If Christopher's own assurances that he's happy and well and enjoying his holiday aren't enough . . ."

Bridget was clenching her teeth in a turmoil of indecision. Indecision wasn't her thing, any more than panic was, but at this juncture it seemed unavoidable. Would she be making matters worse, or better, if she were to reveal to the assembled company that Christopher was right now outside in the road, nowhere near any holiday camp site?

Better for whom? Certainly not for Mervyn. Whatever his motives were for inventing all this rigmarole about the camping trip (and Bridget was only just beginning to speculate on what these motives might be), he certainly wasn't going to be pleased at having his carefully-constructed fiction punctured by the intervention of an uninvited visitor.

Better for Norah, then? Norah had already expressed her grave doubts about the authenticity of the letter. Would it be some satisfaction to her to have her suspicions proved to be well-founded?

Satisfaction of a sort, yes. Everyone likes to be proved right (or so Bridget always supposed), but sometimes there was a heavy price to be paid.

"She was always right, and now she's dead right" – the famous tombstone inscription floated briefly through her consciousness, and increased her uncertainty.

What would Norah gain by having her husband humiliated in front of her friends? He would feel betrayed – furious – and would inevitably take it out on her. And with good reason, too, if he had in fact heard her voicing her suspicions just as he came into the room.

No, the risks involved in telling the truth were too great. Those involved in keeping silent were unknown, and hence less weighty.

None of these thoughts, she trusted, were showing in her face, but all the same they seemed to fill the room.

137

She became suddenly aware of all the other unexpressed thoughts which at this very moment were claiming a share of the enclosed space between these four walls. Mervyn's thoughts, Norah's, even Diana's. The air was thick with thoughts, like some atmospheric pollutant, so concentrated that you could scarcely breathe.

"I think perhaps we should be going," she said politely; and relief swept across the room like a great wind, before it subsided into the normal little conventional remarks incidental to the departure of guests.

Mervyn, courteous and correct to the end, came to see them off at the front door, and for a moment Bridget was filled with trepidation lest he should notice his son lurking under the lamp, and should react by – well who knew how he might react?

But, mercifully, it didn't happen: Christopher was gone. By the time they'd reached the garden gate, and she could peer round the privet hedge, Bridget was sure of this. But her initial feeling of relief was sharply interrupted by Mervyn's voice, close behind them.

"Wait!" he called "Wait a moment. One of you has dropped something." and as they turned, enquiringly, they saw him straightening up from a flower-bed, and coming towards them, holding out a plastic supermarket carrier-bag.

For a moment, all three stared, bewildered. It was Bridget who took the bag – it was surprisingly heavy – and reached inside it. Her fingers encountered metal – a cold, irregular surface. Reaching further in, she pulled the thing out.

It was a hand-gun.

They all stared, bewildered; and on Mervyn's face was a look of actual terror. Was he facing, at last, a long-suppressed awareness of his son's derangement, and its awful unpredictable dangers? Frantically, he seemed to be seeking some alternative and less agonising explanation. While, characteristically, keeping his dignity as he did so.

"Good God!" he exclaimed, "Oh, I *do* apologise, of course it can't be yours! Oh dear, some yobbo, I suppose, planning a break-in and suddenly thinking better of it. Realised he'd been spotted, and reckoned he'd better not be caught with the weapon on him. I'll have to hand it in to the police, I suppose. Oh dear, I *am* sorry! What a parting shock for you!" and after a brief repetition of the conventional remarks appropriate to departing guests, he went indoors, presumably to ring the police about the gun and the attempted break-in.

The three drove home almost in silence, each preoccupied with her own speculations. It was Diana who spoke, just once, towards the end of the journey:

"It's not going to be as easy as I thought," she lamented. "That father's going to be difficult."

You can say that again, thought Bridget, but silently.

Chapter 18

Just as they opened the front door of the flat, the telephone stopped ringing. They stood for a moment looking at each other, in anxious surmise.

"The gun, of course," hazarded Bridget, echoing the thoughts of them all. "I felt sure the police would be getting onto us straight away. They'll want to confirm Mervyn's story about having found it lying in a flower-bed like that. Wrapped in a plastic bag. I mean, it's not a very likely story, is it? On the face of it."

No, it wasn't. And the fact that it had actually happened, that they had all three of them seen it happen, didn't, somehow, make it seem any more plausible.

"You mean they're going to suspect one of *us*? Of having planted it there, or something?" Diana looked from one to the other of her companions. "But that's ridiculous!"

"Of course it is. I'm sure they don't suspect anything of the sort. No – what I'm afraid of – I don't want to upset you, Norah – but I'm afraid the gun must be something to do with Christopher. It *must* be . . . It's too much of a coincidence."

Having gone so far in voicing her suspicions, there seemed nothing for it but to relate in full her encounter with Christopher this evening – which she had so far refrained from doing for fear of upsetting Norah.

But Norah would have to be upset. Probably was already. Sooner or later, she would have to face the facts. It is well-known that facts are easier to face than speculations, and the reason is obvious: facts, of their very nature, are limited to what is possible, whereas anxieties know no such limitations.

"And you see," she finished, "Christopher's delusions about having me in his power and forcing me to commit a murder might have inspired some muddled notion of laying a weapon in my path and 'forcing' me to pick it up. He imagines, you see . . ."

"But how could he get hold of a gun?" protested Diana. "It'd be difficult, you know, even for a nor – well, for an ordinary average sort of boy, and for someone like Christopher . . ."

"It's nothing to do with him, it can't be!" broke in Norah. Christopher wouldn't hurt a fly!"

He would, though. He had. He did. Spiders, anyway. Her voice faltered. Then, recovering herself, she continued: "And anyway it's impossible. Boys get hold of guns through friends, and Christopher hasn't any friends. Besides – Oh, Bridget, you're not going to say all this to the police, are you?"

"About Christopher and the gun?" She paused for a moment. "No-o, I shouldn't think so. I don't think it will be necessary. I mean, it's only my guess that the mad things he said to me about murder might be relevant. The police aren't interested in guesses. They'll only be asking us for facts. Like what time was it, and which bit of the garden did we see Dr Payne picking it up from. That sort of thing. That's all we need tell them. It's all we *can* tell them. We don't actually *know* anything . . ."

"So you won't say anything at all about Christopher, then?" Norah insisted. "I mean, they're sure to ring again. I don't know what I'm going to say, either. I'm Mervyn's wife, I live there, they'll expect me to know a lot more than they'll expect you to –"

"I don't see why . . ." Bridget was beginning; but at that moment the phone went again.

For just a second, they all looked at each other, and no one moved. It was Bridget who first overcame the communal reluctance to face the expected inquisition. She moved briskly across the room, with a clear plan ready of what she was going to say.

And so her first sensation was one of amazement that an unknown official in the police station at Medfield should be addressing her as "darling". Only momentarily, of course; in less than a second she had recognised her father's voice; and had recognised, also, the tinge of reproach in it. Why hadn't she rung home as she had promised, to explain the nature of the emergency that had necessitated her sudden departure yesterday?

"Your mother's been agonising about you all day," he reproached her. "She's been imagining all sorts of ghastly traumas. She didn't like to ring because – and besides, you'd said *you* were going to ring *us* . . . Ah, here she is . . . It's all right, Connie, I've got her! She seems all right. Here, *you* talk to her."

And so here it was again. The old, familiar situation: Bridget's mother longing to hear what her daughter was doing, and Bridget racking her brains to think how not to tell her.

The truth was, of course, that when mothers long to

143

hear what their grown-up daughters are doing, what they really long to hear is that everything is all right: that the daughter isn't unhappy about anything, isn't at risk of losing her job or of having her heart broken.

And of course, at a distance of a hundred miles or so, it is quite easy, with the aid of a very few, very white lies, to assure one's mother that this is in fact the case. Bridget had done this before, and would do so again as necessary. The only trouble with the method was that it was so boring, for both parties.

If only Bridget had felt able to tell her mother what had *really* happened yesterday, what a fascinating conversation they could have had. Ironically, it would have been just the kind of exciting gossip that her mother loved best – so long as the heroine of the drama was anyone else in the whole world other than her own daughter.

It was a difficult story to make boring, but she managed it. Her mother had to be protected from the truth because of the intensity of her concern. Of her love, actually, to give the thing its proper name. It is love that creates the barriers between parents and grown-up children. Indifference, or even hate, might be less inhibiting.

As soon as she realised that it wasn't the police that Bridget was talking to, it also occurred to Norah that it couldn't have been. Because how would the police have found out their telephone number – or their address – Norah having kept her whereabouts so carefully secret? Or, she now wondered uneasily, might Diana have inadvertently revealed it during that first interview with Christopher? "If you have any questions, you can get hold of me here," she might

144

have said, handing him her card automatically. And then Christopher could have handed it to his father – or simply left it lying around. Might Christopher and his father have actually discussed the television project? With what result? Were they, in fact, talking to one another at all?

She must think, think. Murmuring something about having an early night, she retired to her room. She closed the door, drew the curtains, and lay down full length on the bed, closing her eyes. She didn't even have the light on – what was the point when her eyes were shut? She could think better that way; felt she could, anyway.

In considering the implications of Mervyn's forging of that letter – and she was almost one hundred percent certain that it *was* a forgery – it was necessary first to ask herself how she had *expected* him to behave, once he was left alone with total responsibility for his schizophrenic son. Deliberately, and after careful consideration, she had landed him in this situation. Her idea had been that once he was on his own, face to face with the boy's bizarre and frightening behaviour, he would be forced to recognise that something was wrong. He would be forced to swallow his professional pride and let it be known that he, a top-ranking psychotherapist, a specialist in mental illness, had a son who was mentally ill. The humiliation of it was something he had been warding off for years, as Norah knew to her cost. He had been warding off not only the humiliation of the facts becoming known to his colleagues and patients, but, perhaps even more, the humiliation of knowing them fully himself. His near-crazy attempts to interpret his son's behaviour as being within the range of normality had been no mere pretence: it had been genuine, a last-ditch effort to make himself *see* the behaviour as normal.

Norah understood all this; she had understood it, all too well, for a long time. To understand all *may* be to forgive all, she mused; but that was not the same as being able to put up with it. For months and years, Norah had put up with being the accursed and derided messenger, the buffer between Mervyn and his son's worsening insanity. All the time she was there, in the house, it was possible for her husband to claim that it was *her* anxieties, *her* neurotic behaviour, that forced their son to put up psychological defences against her, taking the form sometimes, of bizarre behaviour. And, of course, Dr Mervyn Payne's high professional qualifications made it hard for anyone – let alone his wife – to query any of his psychological pronouncements. Especially when, at some level, he believed them himself; he had forced himself, trained himself over the long months to believe them. To have believed otherwise would have been intolerable.

Norah understood all this. Of course she did. She just couldn't put up with it; it was as simple as that.

Right, then. So what had she *expected* would happen if she succeeded in forcing her husband to confront something that was intolerable to him? Really, actually intolerable? What *did* people do when the intolerable became the inescapable?

On and off, over the years, Norah had occasionally wondered if, just possibly, her husband might be right, and that her own neurotic and irrational attitudes were at the root of the problem. This thought had briefly re-surfaced in her mind yesterday, when she had found

146

Christopher apparently so well and so rational after her ten-day absence. The possibility that his problems had been, after all, her own doing had filled her both with dismay and with wild hope. If the fault actually *was* in herself, then it was within her power to do something about it, if only by removing herself from his life.

But subsequent events had put paid to all this. Christopher *wasn't* better. He had merely succeeded (as is not uncommon with schizophrenics) in putting on a good show for outsiders. But now, today, he was as bad as ever. Worse, as the encounter with Bridget amply proved. Norah had listened, with mounting apprehension, to Bridget's account. 'I can *make* you commit murder," he'd said to her; and Norah had felt herself growing numb with fear. Not about Bridget – that was obviously nonsense, but about her son's revelling in thoughts of murder. This was a new symptom, and it had a sinister quality that had never been in evidence before. With thoughts of murder churning in his brain, and with his powers of reasoning so deranged, what might he not do next? And where did that gun come into it? A gun, in a plastic bag, shoved carelessly into a clump of foliage – this, surely, could not be the work of a sane person? In spite of her assertion that the gun could have nothing to do with Christopher, she had not really believed her own words. That it should appear so soon after the murder threat seemed beyond the bounds of coincidence.

Had Mervyn, too, suspected that the gun must be something to do with his crazy son? Had Christopher been talking to his father in the same sort of way as he'd been talking to Bridget? If Mervyn did indeed suspect that his son's illness was now escalating to a stage when he might become violent, then this would be some sort of explanation of the forged letter. It might – might it not? – be a father's clumsy and desperate attempt to provide his son with an alibi for whatever deed of violence might be pending.

In the midst of their dark and terrifying family situation, it was a little bit touching, was it not, that Mervyn should be trying so frantically to provide his son with an alibi for an as yet uncommitted crime. It seemed that, in his proud and desperate way, Mervyn *loved* his son.

Was it the real son that he loved, the sick, mad one? Or was it still the imaginary one, the long-vanished little boy, so brilliant at maths and music?

Chapter 19

By Monday morning; life at the flat was rapidly going back to normal. It occurred to Bridget that they had probably been over-reacting to the situation. The discovery of a hand-gun in a flower-bed in a suburban garden had certainly struck them as a remarkable event, and somewhat sinister; but perhaps the police wouldn't see it like that at all. This sort of thing was probably all in a day's work to them; maybe dozens of guns turned up in odd places every week and were merely added to an existing list of similar findings, only to re-surface if some crime of violence in the neighbourhood made one or other of these abandoned guns seem relevant.

Bridget felt relieved, for her own sake as well as Norah's, that no new crisis seemed to be imminent. Other people's troubles are time-consuming, and Bridget was exceptionally busy this week. She had two international conferences outside London to prepare for and, more immediately, a session of unpredictable length with a Polish philosopher who was querying a number of points in her translation of his article on Linguistic Analysis and the Falsification Principle. Her English version did not seem to him to do justice to the force and vigour of the prose with which he was demolishing the arguments of his philosophical opponents in all parts of Europe as well as in Poland.

And indeed he might have a point. She had been aware at the time of translating his sentences rather over-literally, and without a proper grasp of what he was driving at. Perhaps she should do a bit more background reading – Wittgenstein and Popper and so forth – before embarking on a re-draft. A long and concentrated evening's work would be needed, anyway, and she hoped there would be no interruptions. Surely she was entitled to a bit of peace and quiet after having devoted almost the whole weekend to Norah and her problems? She realised, of course, that the ebb and flow of a person's problems couldn't be expected to dovetail precisely with the amount of leisure her friends had for hearing about them, but surely *something* could be worked out? Shouldn't there be some sort of unwritten rule about it, she wondered? If *I've* got an important deadline to meet by Tuesday midday, then *you* must keep your broken heart on ice until Tuesday after lunch. Ideally, you must arrange not to break up with your lover *until* Tuesday. Or let your cat get run over, or whatever. That way, friendship can flourish, *and* we all get on with earning a living. That's how it would be, in an ideal world.

And Bridget could create a temporarily ideal world of this kind, by retiring to her own room, shutting the door, and letting the others answer the telephone. Diana was good about this, she quite enjoyed telling effortless white lies about Bridget being out, confident that Bridget would do the same for her, should the occasion (such as Alistair turning up unexpectedly) arise. They were well-practised, too, in taking messages for each other, with commendable accuracy and discretion.

150

It was unfortunate, though, that on this particular evening Professor Brzozowski should choose to call. His message, conserning his article for the Journal of Linguistic Analysis, delivered in a heavy East European accent, defeated even Diana; and the desperate urgency of it, which he managed to convey despite the language barrier, was such as to force her to summon Bridget from her seclusion.

A question about the nature of Reality and its relationship to human thought-processes might strike some as not being particularly urgent, the question having been debated continuously for at least three thousand years, but this was not how it struck Professor Brzozowski. For had he not solved the problem once and for all in his Linguistic Analysis article? Was it not a tragic loss to mankind that this once-and-for-all solution should not be laid before them in its perfect clarity? Properly translated, it would provide irrefutable arguments in favour of this interpretation of the Universe and mankind's place in it, provided it reached the Editorial Department of the Linguistic Analysis Journal by 9.00 on Friday morning.

The conversation was a protracted one, as might have been expected, and in the course of it Bridget suffered the additional annoyance of registering, out of the corner of her eye, the arrival of Alistair. He was carrying a bottle of red wine and an evening paper, but all the same managed to have a hand free to tweak her hair as he passed; managed too to murmur "What-ho, Smarty-pants?" into her ear, just as she was trying to make out the title of an abstruse Polish journal from which the professor was quoting.

By the time the laborious interchange was over a

meal was ready. Roast chicken, with all the trimmings. Diana (whose turn it was to cook) must have known that Alistair would be coming, though she hadn't warned any of them. No reason why she should, of course, but all the same . . . Bridget saw her evening of concentrated work fast vanishing as she found herself drawn into the after-dinner conversation. Norah had retired to her room almost as soon as the meal was over, which left Diana a free hand to make a colourful story, for Alistair's benefit, of Sunday's alarms and excursions.

He listened, as always, with a judicious mixture of scorn for female gossip and an avid lust for every last detail. His eager questioning elicited from Diana more, perhaps, than a strict regard for confidentiality should have allowed her to divulge; but it couldn't really do any harm, could it? – especially as her every revelation was conscientiously prefaced by "Don't let it go any further, will you . . .?"

He was fascinated by the story of the gun in the flower-bed, and expressed surprise that they weren't all three of them in prison already.

"Because it's in the paper tonight," he informed them, gesturing towards the copy of the *Standard*, which by now lay around dismembered on the carpet, as papers were liable to do when Alistair had been reading them, "It's in the paper that there *has* been a murder in this benighted Medfield of yours. Well, on Medfield Common, anyway. I suppose that must be somewhere near. A body's been found in some undergrowth, and a hand-gun near it. Your cock-and-bull story about a gun in a flower-bed will be on the front page of every newspaper

152

tomorrow. It'll be on the police computer already, and they'll . . ."

"Oh, but darling, it *was* in the flower-bed!" cried Diana. "We all saw Mervyn picking it up, didn't we, Bridget? It's *not* a cock-and-bull story. It's the truth!"

"Sweetie, whatever's that got to do with it? You don't really believe that the mere truth is going to be relevant, do you? You've been watching too much T.V.. Correction: you've been *producing* too much T.V., and it's turned your little head. I've kept telling you all along that it was going to land you in trouble, now haven't I? It stands to reason that anyone whose job it is to involve herself, day in and day out, in situations of on-going catastrophe – she's bound to get the blame sooner or later. It's like social workers: if some scoundrel beats his child to death, it's not his fault, it's the fault of the social worker who didn't stop him. And it's just the same with T.V. T.V. these days is simply a gigantic social worker who hasn't had to go through any training. It not only has to remedy every known evil, but has to make evil amusing as well. Your trouble, Di dear, is that you're too kind-hearted. Your actual job is to be the life and soul of every disaster, but you let your sympathies get in the way. You empathise. You worry about people's feelings. Now, if it was our Bridget" – he threw a mocking glance in her direction – "a lady so clever and so highly educated that she understands nothing whatsoever about people's feelings . . ."

"Oh, but darling, that's not fair!" cried Diana. "Bridget *does* . . ."

"Oh, all right, all right! Alistair mimicked cringing terror, shutting his eyes and pressing himself deep into the sofa cushions, "I'll withdraw the charge. Put it this

153

way: Bridget understands other people's feelings all right, she just doesn't think they're of any importance. Is that better?"

He half-opened his eyes, to see how Bridget was taking all this.

She wasn't looking at him at all; seemed, indeed, not to be listening, busying herself with piecing together the maltreated evening paper, sorting the pages neatly into their original correct order

"I don't see anything about the murder," she remarked, when she'd finished. "Are you sure you didn't dream it?"

"*Dream* it? Good God, when I dream, I dream of better things than that, I can tell you!" His attempt to meet Bridget's eye with flirtatious innuendo was a failure, for she was still scanning the paper intently.

"It's only the Stop Press, so far," he pointed out. "It caught my eye when I was checking on the Stock Market, and I must say I chuckled a bit. Do you remember I moved the car round the corner because I didn't want the whole neighbourhood noticing me sitting there in the same place for hours? "Supposing there's a murder around here," I said, and you thought I was joking. Well, to be honest, *I* thought I was joking, too. But I wasn't, was I? It was probably happening right then, while I said it!"

He sounded pleased with hiself, rather proud, as people are when they turn out by chance to have been right about something.

By this time Bridget had tracked down the item.

"It doesn't say much," she remarked; "Just that enquiries are . . ." She broke off abruptly: "Why, *Norah*! We thought you'd gone to bed!"

154

For a moment, Bridget felt as guilty as a school-child caught cheating. How much had Norah heard? Did it *matter* how much she'd heard? In her present state of nerves, *everything* upset her, and so this would too. Unobtrusively, Bridget slipped the neatly-folded paper out of sight behind the sofa, and set herself, under Alistair's cynical gaze, to change the subject. With deliberate perversity – or so it seemed – he tried to foil her every attempt at an innocuous topic. Holidays in the South of France? At once he had to remind them of the couple who had been shot dead there last summer. Recent proposed changes in Primary Education? Immediately he referred to primary schools in America where pupils were searched for knives and guns as they came in every morning. Autumn pruning of roses? Hadn't there been a rose bush right there where they found the gun?

Bridget gave up; and was greatly relieved when Norah, after hovering uneasily around for a while, said goodnight for a second time and left the room.

In her absence it seemed opportune to switch on the news in case there was any mention of the murder; and sure enough there was. The police were conducting investigations, and would appreciate assistance from the public. If anyone had noticed anything unusual in the vicinity . . . had been walking in the wooded area of Common recently . . . had noticed anything suspicious. "Any clue, however seemingly trivial, may be just the one that we are looking for . . . ."

The news came to an end, and the party broke up: Alistair and Diana went off to their king-size bed and Bridget returned to her desk, where she settled down to her much-interrupted studies.

So absorbed was she that she did not notice the faint, tiny sounds which Norah could not help making as she crept out of her bedroom and back into the sitting-room. She had waited, sleepless, staring into the dark, until she felt quite sure that the others were finally settled in their rooms: and now, at last, was her chance. Furtive as any burglar, she tiptoed barefoot across the landing, across the soft, pale sitting-room carpet that muffled her every step, and retrieved the evening paper from behind the sofa, where she had observed Bridget stowing it. She did not dare open it out straight away, but tiptoed back with it to the seclusion of her room; and even there she found herself taking obsessional care to avoid rustling the pages as she searched. Just in case anyone was still awake. Just in case anyone was listening through the wall.

As a result of all these precautions it took her some minutes to locate the item from which her friends had so obviously been trying to shield her: and when she did, she read it not once, but three or four times, short though it was.

"It doesn't say much," Bridget had remarked; and certainly, on the face of it, this was the case. But for Norah it said enough. She hadn't really needed to read it over and over again like this, for she had known at once, after a single glance, what it was that had happened.

Chapter 20

Bridget had to be up early the next morning, before it was light. She was surprised, when she entered the kitchen, to find that Diana was already there. She was leaning dreamily against the counter, while the electric kettle boiled alongside. Luckily, it was the kind which in the end switches itself off when confronted by this degree of inattention; and this it duly did, just as Diana began to speak.

"Oh, Bridget, such wonderful news!" she exclaimed; and then: "Oh – all right! *You* make your coffee first, if you like. I'm feeling just too blissful to bother about coffee, I really am!"

Too blissful to bother about coffee? Spooning instant into her own mug, Bridget silently toyed with one or two guesses. An offer of a top job in one of the new channels? Or had Alistair at last popped the question? Or – and here Bridget's heart sank – could it be that . . .?

Yes, it could. Diana was five days overdue. "I didn't say anything before, because I was afraid of bringing it on – you know, tempting Providence!" she exulted. "I was scared last night that it might be starting – but it wasn't. Not a sign. Oh, Bridget, I'm so *thrilled*! Five days! It's never been as late as this before!"

It had, though. Bridget could remember it all too well. Much though she deplored her friend's determination to have a baby regardless of circumstances, she dreaded still more the wailing and gnashing of teeth which would engulf the whole household when, after five, seven – even eight days, the premature hopes would all be washed away.

That's how it had been last time, anyway, and though Bridget had done her best to sympathise, and to hide her own extreme relief that the threatened upheaval in their comfortable lives was not, after all, going to materialise, it had still been a traumatic time. Diana's disappointment and depression had lingered on for – how long was it? Days? Weeks? Too long, anyway. And an additional annoyance was that Alistair, the *fons et origo* of the whole business, had been elaborately spared all suffering and annoyance. Diana had revealed to him nothing either of her initial hopes nor of their subsequent collapse. That he would have been put out and dismayed by the idea of Diana's pregnancy was of course beyond question. Even Diana herself was in no doubt about this: but she clung pertinaciously to the theory that he could come to like the idea once he got used to it ("Men do, you know"); and that he would *adore* the baby once it was there.

He wouldn't, of that Bridget felt absolutely sure: though whether he would find the inconveniences of fatherhood so great as to warrant dislodging himself from a comfortable second home, this was more doubtful. If Diana could somehow protect him from broken nights, interrupted meals, and all the other inconveniences of parenthood, he might well stay around. Diana would interpret this as "adoring the baby". He wouldn't be unkind to it: as he himself had pointed out on other occasions, being unkind to people was inordinately time-consuming: it always ended in some kind of a fuss, and a busy man had better things to do than to get involved in fusses.

With these thoughts coursing through her mind, Bridget found it difficult to congratulate Diana whole-heartedly, but she did her best; made a second cup of coffee and set it in front of her friend, and only then ventured on a carefully-worded warning to the effect that five days wasn't all *that* late; it could happen to anybody – "Especially if they keep thinking about it all the time, the way you do."

"Oh, but Bridget, it's not just that! I've got a tingling feeling in my breasts, too, and that's one of the very first signs, everyone says so. And there's more even than that – I don't know how to explain it, but I can *feel* the baby inside me! Truly I can! Yes, I know it's less than a millimeter long, I *know* all that, all the scientific stuff, of course I do; but there's something else as well – something beyond science. It's a *person*, already. I can feel it is. It's *my* baby, and I love it, love it, love it . . .!"

"Oh, Bridget, this baby is going to be loved so much, so much! Whatever happens, love like this will make up to him for *anything*!"

In hopes of hiding the luke-warmness of her response to her friend's ecstasies, Bridget got up from her stool and went across the room to pull up the blinds. By now, it was growing light, and above the roofs opposite a pale yellow dawn, flecked with wisps of cloud, was creeping up the sky. For nearly a minute she stood there, her back to Diana, trying to adjust her thoughts – or rather her feelings – to this new development.

It was a *nuisance*. This, she realised to her shame, was her predominant feeling. And it was especially a nuisance right now, when they were already coping with a major irritant in the form of Norah and her problems; and just when Bridget herself was planning, this very morning, to involve herself yet deeper in the unhappy events at Medfield. Not because she wanted to – far from it – but because, in her view, it was a civic duty, and inescapable.

Would this be Norah's view, too, when she heard what Bridget had done? Or would she see it not as a civic duty at all, but as black treachery?

For Bridget would have to tell her – of course she would. For one thing, Norah would be bound to hear about it in the end; and for another it was only decent, it was common honesty, to put her in the picture.

As soon as possible after the deed was done, she must seek an opportunity to talk to Norah on her own.

The opportunity came quite early in the afternoon, Diana was at the studio, and expected to be there until quite late – concentrating on the job in hand, one hoped, and not drifting about in her precarious dream of bliss – and Alistair had taken himself off, and with any luck wouldn't re-appear until tomorrow. And so when Bridget arrived back at the flat, having had a quick lunch at the station buffet, she found Norah on her own, as she had hoped. Or half-hoped, anyway; the encounter wasn't one to which she was looking forward.

Did it make it easier, or harder, that Norah looked already as if she was bracing herself for just such an

160

uncomfortable interview as Bridget had in store for her? She was sitting on the very edge of the sofa in the large, light sitting room, and seemed to be doing absolutely nothing; just staring through the long windows at an expanse of winter sky.

She looked up, warily, as Bridget crossed the room towards her, but did not speak: not even to say "Hullo", or to respond to Bridget's own greeting. And so, without preamble, Bridget pulled forward one of the straight-backed dining chairs (this was not an occasion for lounging in comfort), settled herself in it facing Norah, and began.

"Look, Norah, I'm afraid this may be going to upset you, but I *must* tell you, it's only fair . . ." And she went on to relate, in detail, the interview she had had with the police this morning, and the account she had given them of her bizarre encounter with Christopher on Sunday evening.

"I *had* to tell them, you see," she explained. "I don't think you were watching the news with us last night, but an appeal was issued to the general public to report to the police any unusual circumstance they might have noticed recently in the Medfield area. And it *was* an unusual circumstance, that encounter I had with Christopher. And so was the finding of the gun in your front garden, I told them about that, too. I *had* to.

"I'm sorry, Norah; I know how you must feel. Christopher is your son, and you must hate to have any suspicion thrown on him, but it just can't be avoided. You have to help the police in a murder case, it's an absolute duty. And, you know, it may easily turn out to be nothing to do with Christopher at all. It's more

161

than likely that he was just fantasising about murders when I was with him. Well, he fantasises all the time, doesn't he? And if that's all there was to it, then the police will soon find it out and eliminate him from their enquiries. That's much the most likely thing, when you come to think of it.

"But, Norah, suppose the very worst happens: suppose it *does* turn out that the gun your husband found was put there by Christopher? And suppose Christopher did, somehow, in some kind of deluded state, shoot someone as part of his fantasy? Even then, Norah, it won't mean that anything very terrible will happen to him. They will discover at once that he is mentally unstable, and he won't be treated as an ordinary criminal. He certainly won't go to prison, he'll be sent for psychiatric assessment to be followed by treatment. Residential treatment, in some sort of hospital. And, Norah, wouldn't that honestly be the very best thing that could happen to him? You've told us that for years you've been trying to get his father to face the fact that the boy needs expert treatment; and this way, don't you see, he'll be getting that expert treatment, whether his father wishes it or not. There will be no way at all that your husband will be able to prevent it; it'll be out of his hands.

"Think about it, Norah. Obviously, no one could have wanted it to come about in this tragic way, but all the same it could – it really could – be the very best thing to have happened to Christopher. It could give him a real chance of recovery . . ."

Only now did Bridget realise that she had been talking, talking, talking for the best part of half an hour, and that Norah had not, as yet, spoken a single word. She

162

had been watching Bridget's face rather as one might watch a play on television; a passive spectator, to whom the outcome of the drama was of no significance.

Bridget paused, waiting for some response, and when none was forthcoming, she continued: "Well, that's the worst-case scenario, I suppose. The other one – and far the most likely one, really, is that Christopher had nothing to do with the murder. Absolutely nothing. In which case the evidence will clear him. It will show conclusively that he didn't do it."

And now, at long last, Norah seemed to rouse herself.

"That's right," she said. "He didn't do it. He couldn't have, you see. Christopher is the one who is dead."

Chapter 21

Once again Norah was lying on her bed, sleepless, dry-eyed, staring at nothing. This time, though, it was not even dark. She had drawn the curtains across against the last of the afternoon sun, but of course sunlight, the light of the whole earth, was not to be kept at bay so easily. Through the heavy folds of brown velour a misty, luminous visibility permeated the room, obscuring everything, yet hiding nothing. Even that uncomfortable picture of a slumped female figure – too impersonal to be called a woman – perched on a lop-sided chair, could still be discerned, squareish, darkish, against the lighter background of the wall.

To an observer, if there had been one, Norah would have appeared totally relaxed; but actually she was intensely busy trying to feel something. Anything.

She was in shock, of course, that numbness-inducing shock of bereavement, that stops the tortured emotions from functioning for a merciful few hours, or even days.

But this numbness of Norah's was something more than the dead hand of shock. Norah knew it was, and she struggled against it as one struggles to wake from a nightmare. Or would she be waking *into* a nightmare, and not out of one at all, when her faculties finally returned?

It was more than twelve hours now since she had learned that Christopher was dead. Had had it confirmed, rather, for even as she'd scanned that stop-press item in the paper, she'd had the curious sensation that she'd known it all along: had known for certain, through all the long years, even during her son's bright, successful early childhood, that this was exactly how it was going to end.

It wasn't true, of course. She hadn't known anything of the sort, how could she? It just felt like that, now. Perhaps it always does, when something like this happens?

Shock, again?

Somehow, she must try to get to grips with herself, to take in what had happened. She would have to *think*; and she now discovered, with vague surprise, that though emotion of any kind whatsoever had withdrawn to some place far beyond her reach, her brain itself was still working – working, indeed, with unusual clarity.

It was quite clear now, looking at events dispassionately, that the whole thing had been her fault. Not that she felt any guilt about this – guilt, like all other emotions, had gone beyond her reach for the time being, and therefore could neither trouble her nor distort her judgement. Right now, Norah was able to see, perhaps more clearly than she ever would again, exactly what had happened, and why.

It had been her decision to run away from home that had begun it all. At the time, it had seemed not only a justifiable, but almost an inevitable decision, the only option open to her. She'd been at the end of her tether, no longer able to cope with Christopher's ever-worsening delusions. And the thing that had made her difficult task quite impossible had been her husband's obsessive refusal to accept that anything was wrong with his son. He just couldn't take it. It was not only his professional pride as a distinguished psychiatrist at stake, but even more damaging, it was his pride in himself. That he, Dr Mervyn Payne, so handsome, so brilliant, so successful, so endowed with every desirable quality for handing on to the future generation, should be the one to have fathered so damaged a child – this was something he couldn't endure.

He simply couldn't face it.

So, I'll *make* him face it, Norah had decided on that fatal day. I'll leave him to cope with Christopher on his own for a while, then he'll *have* to recognise the truth. He'll *have* to do something about it.

And her ruse had worked. It had worked beyond her wildest dreams. Mervyn *had* recognised the truth. He *had* done something about it. He had shot the boy dead. Better a dead son than a non-stop burden of humiliation, a daily and hourly source of shame for the rest of his natural life.

Did he expect to get away with it? Of course he did. The same overweening pride and arrogance that had driven him to the deed would sustain his belief in his own power of evading the consequences. His high professional status, his agile intelligence, his knowledge of legal procedures would all be on his side. The body hadn't been identified yet – perhaps it never would be. Perhaps misleading documents planted in the pockets would set the police off on a false trail – perhaps to some distant part of the country. In identifying an unknown body, surely the standard procedure would be to match it up with the lists of Missing Persons held

167

on police computers all over the country? Christopher would appear on no such list, for Mervyn had already taken the precaution of concocting that phoney letter to indicate that the boy was away on a camping holiday during the relevant week. Other letters would doubtless be contrived to cover subsequent weeks, until local interest had died down. The fact that Christopher had no friends would assist matters: no one would miss him, or come looking for him, or invite him out anywhere. His tragic life, now over, would quickly fade into oblivion. Should the need occasionally arise, his father could shrug off his absence with some plausible story. The boy was eighteen, quite old enough to be off on his own, like so many of his contemporaries, on some overland jaunt to some remote part of the world. Very popular, this sort of thing: who would bother to query it? Or even be in the least degree interested? Who *is* interested in hearing about what other people's eighteen-year-olds are doing?

The boy's mother, of course, would be interested; but had she not already seen the letter describing the alleged camping holiday? Other similarly forged letters could follow, and references to occasional phone calls from foreign parts. Norah, having providentially left home, could hardly wonder why it was that *she* was never the one to take these calls.

Something like that would be Mervyn's strategy, anyway. And none of it would – or indeed could – have come about if Norah had stayed at her post instead of running away. She could still be there, suffering, agonising, and at her wit's end; and Christopher could still be alive.

It was all her doing, all of it; and yet still she felt

no guilt. Nor grief. Nor fear. Nor shame. Absolutely nothing.

When she woke, it was already quite dark. Sitting up and twitching aside one corner of the heavy curtain, she peered down onto the empty street below, quiet under the widely-spaced street lights. Not a pedestrian in sight anywhere, and only the occasional car.

It must be quite late, the rush-hour well and truly over. Although this was by no means a main road, traffic was fairly continuous for most of the day. Perhaps it was already after midnight? Or maybe it was that other quiet stretch of a London evening, the hour between nine and ten when the working population is back from work, and when the evening revellers have already set off but are not yet due to return.

At this point in her musings, Norah noticed a car approaching . . . slowing down. Yes, a yellow car, as far as one could judge in these deceptive lights. Yes, Diana's car; it drew up outside their door. Diana, slender and elegant in some kind of glittering garment under her dark cloak, was descending from the passenger seat. Diana was good at getting out of cars, she accomplished it not clumsily, effortfully, like most women, but lightly, easily, like a ballet dancer; while from the other door, not in the least like a ballet dancer, Alistair heaved himself, the balding forefront of his cranium gleaming in the cruel greenish light.

Footsteps. Doors opening and closing . . . and now the sound of voices from the sitting-room. No, not proper voices, it must be the radio. No, the television. The ten o'clock news.

News. There would be something about Christopher

169

for sure, though of course they wouldn't know it was Christopher. The body still hadn't been identified.

Or had it? Norah scrambled to her feet, curiosity suddenly overcoming reluctance. A strangely pure kind of reluctance it was, quite unmixed with distress or apprehension. It was as if she was about to hear the next instalment of an intriguing story about someone else, nothing to do with her; and as she slid into the sitting-room and joined the other two in front of the television set, the level of her interest in this new murder mystery was more or less on a par with theirs. She was curious, as they were, to learn whether any progress had been made in identifying the victim.

But it didn't really seem to matter. Norah felt no more personally concerned about the subject than her companions.

Less concerned, probably; after all, she already knew the answer.

No real progress had been made. The stub of a long-distance coach-ticket found in the dead man's anorak pocket suggested that his home might be somewhere around Tyneside. Perhaps (it was hypothesised), he might have come south looking for work?

Briefly, Norah wondered how Mervyn had come by such a ticket-stub? But maybe it wasn't all that difficult. Maybe you just had to hang about the coach terminal keeping your eye on the litter-bins. Not that the question bothered her much. She found herself becoming genuinely interested in the idle chat and speculation that arose between her companions as soon as the News itself had been switched off.

"Lucky old Mervyn, that he found that gun and handed it in *before* all this happened!" remarked

170

Alistair, stretching out his legs to their usual obstructive length across the carpet. "I say, darling, how about a nightcap after our heavy evening?" But Diana, anticipating his wishes, was already diving into the glass-fronted cupboard where the drinks were kept.

Whisky, of course, was what they were having, and Norah shook her head dumbly when it came to her turn. She didn't like whisky, and anyway, for some reason her mouth was terribly dry already, without making it worse with alcohol. Besides, she wasn't really there, they only thought she was because they could see her. Really she was high up some- where, a fly on the ceiling, listening but not par- taking. It was interesting that the two of them took for granted that Mervyn had in fact handed in the gun as he'd said he would. Of course he hadn't; he had just wanted some witnesses to confirm that he'd intended to do so, just in case the question should ever arise.

Which it almost certainly wouldn't have. Now, though, it probably would, as a result of Bridget's precipitate revelations to the police. But of course Mervyn wouldn't as yet know anything about this. He would still be feeling pretty secure.

Norah's two companions were by now side by side on the sofa, and the speculations were continuing in the cosy, leisurely fashion characteristic of the non- implicated when discussing someone else's tragedy.

"And of course," Diana was musing, "It may easily turn out to be suicide, you know what the young are. Shot through the head at point-blank range . . . they say that's the way men usually do it, whereas women usually go for pills. And it's true, you know. I remember, when

171

we were doing the Samaritans, they were saying that 80% of . . ."

"Heartless little monster!" Alistair interposed affectionately, pulling her towards him. "It's all just goggle-fodder to you, isn't it? Murder, rape, suicide, you-name-it, to you it's merely . . ."

"Oh, darling, that's not *fair!*" cried Diana, pulling away from him, half-laughing, half offended. "You *know* it means more to me than that! Don't you remember I came home actually *crying* after I'd interviewed that poor girl's mother? That fifteen-year-old, I mean, who died after taking thirty aspirins? Not nearly enough to kill you normally, as she probaby knew, but she was just unlucky. It was a cry for help – suicides so often are. Maybe that's what it was with this poor chap on the Common – a cry for help. We don't know."

"We do know," remarked Alistair. "We know perfectly well. A bullet through the ,brain at point-blank range – it doesn't sound like a cry for help to me. It sounds like someone who at least meant business.

"But *whose* business? Because of course murder, too, can be a cry for help: had you thought of that? Why don't you set *that* up as an idea for the goggle-ghouls? Make a change from all these boring old rapes and battered wives and ill-used Carers –" Reaching for the bowl of nuts, he searched among them, avid as a squirrel, for one of the last remaining cashews that still lurked among the salted peanuts.

"Which reminds me", he continued, "Are you still expecting to poke your weaselly little nose into that unlucky household in Murder-ville? A bit accident-prone, aren't they? I mean, you're always saying that

172

you don't want anything that happens to your interview-
ees to be your fault: your Jeremy or whoever would be
onto you like a ton of bricks, isn't that so?"

"Oh, Alistair, *shush!*" She gave him a sharp nudge,
reminding him that Norah might well be upset by
such talk. Reminding him, indeed, that Norah was
still there.

Which she wasn't, of course; but Diana couldn't be
expected to know that; when there, before her very
eyes Norah was sitting, small and hunched and silent
in the depths of the big armchair. And at the same
time, non-existent though she was, Norah found herself
still able to wish that Diana hadn't so hastily silenced
her inconsiderate and tactless lover, to wish, indeed,
that she had actually answered his question. Was she
planning to go ahead with her interviews? It would be
the father who answered the door to her now, and if
she cross-questioned him too pertinaciously about the
whereabouts of his son, would she come out of the
interview alive?

Norah tried to care, one way or the other. She longed
to care. If only she could care, then that would give
her the strength to warn Diana, which of course she
ought to do.

But by now the two lovers were leaning together on
the sofa, teasing, whispering, and for Norah to creep
silently from the room was surely the appropriate
thing to do.

Chapter 22

It must have been in the early hours of the morning when Norah came back into her body and found she had recovered the power to feel. It was almost a physical sensation: it rushed through her veins like a blood-transfusion, like an intravenous drip, and she realised for the first time that her son actually was dead. She had known it, of course, for a good many hours, but now she realised it as well, and the grief that had been quietly waiting for her all this time surged over her, taking her breath away.

Grief for what? For whom? For the broken, damaged travesty of a person that Christopher had become? Or for the bright, precocious little boy, so full of quaint ideas, so passionate for facts, any sort of facts, about anything? A lovely little boy, so strong and handsome and eager, a constant joy to his parents.

A little boy long vanished, and the grief at his loss dissipated, bit by bit, over the long dark years that had followed.

What was left? Staring into the darkness, Norah found herself face to face with the nature of grief itself: not just the strange, ambivalent kind of grief that she herself was experiencing, but any grief, anywhere, for anyone.

Grief, she mused, is like a dark room, intermittently lit by a torch turned this way and that, lighting up one by one all the things that now you need not worry about any more. That long-dreaded telephone call? It has come, it is over, it will never come again. You know the worst now. Never again will you have to lift the receiver, sick with dread lest just this very thing may have happened. It *has* happened. It can't happen again. That sudden cry of terror from out in the street? It can't be *your* child. Not this time. Not ever again. That shriek of brakes as a lorry thunders by? Nothing to do with you. Not this time.

Christopher not home yet? No longer that nail-biting anxiety – Where is he? – What is he up to? Of course he's not home yet, how could he be? He's dead. And then that terrifying article in some medical journal about burnt-out schizophrenics in their forties and fifties; you can forget about that now, for Christopher will never be forty or fifty: never be a burnt-out schizophrenic with no one left to look after him.

No more worries at all. No more fears. No more kidding myself he's getting better while watching him get worse.

The simultaneous lifting of all these burdens, so vast, so intractable, beyond all counting, was overwhelming. The sensation of weightlessness, for which astronauts undergo months of training, was upon her suddenly, effortlessly, after no training whatsoever, and no relevant skills.

Beyond the heavy folds of the curtains a streaky yellowish dawn was breaking, but Norah did not see it. The distant roar of the awakening city was gathering strength, but Norah did not hear it. She was standing

176

on a high hill, with a confused and distant landscape spread at her feet and a warm wind pulsing in her ears; and at her side stood Christopher. Which Christopher? The eager, promising, lovable little boy? Or the tall and handsome youth with the ruined mind and the sly, too-brilliant eyes?

Somehow, he was both. Tall and handsome, certainly, and yet calling her "Mummy", as he hadn't done for years and years and years.

"Look, Mummy! Look! I'm King of the World!" he cried, and with his arms stretched out in triumph and with his fair hair blown by the wind across his forehead, that was exactly what he looked like – King of the World.

She must have slept for several hours, because when she woke it was bright day, the low winter sun almost at its zenith, and the flat was empty.

Well, it would be. The others both had jobs to go to, and though their hours were irregular, they were both usually out for most of the day.

Norah was glad. She didn't want to face either of them at the moment. Conversation with Diana would be awkward and embarrassing because Diana didn't know that Christopher was dead. With Bridget it would be embarrassing because she did.

It had been embarrassing already, in fact. When, yesterday, Norah had blurted out the tragic fact, hitherto known only to herself, Bridget had been visibly at a loss. "Oh, God!" you could see her thinking, "What on earth does one say to a bereaved mother? You can't just say you're sorry, and walk away . . . probably the right thing to do is to put your arms around her . . ." Norah could actually *feel* the revulsion that

177

had shuddered through her companion at the thought, and she had understood it well. An exchange of duty-hugging between people who aren't particularly fond of each other can be excruciating. It was awful; and who knew to what heights the embarrassment might have escalated, had not the telephone mercifully intervened.

It didn't matter who the call was for, or who answered it, for while one was doing so, the other could escape, and so bring the painful session to an end.

An end to the embarrassment, perhaps; but now, looking back on the episode, it dawned on Norah that something more than embarrassment might have been at stake, and she felt stirrings of a new uneasiness.

Why – why – had she been so imprudent as to tell Bridget anything at all of what she knew? She hadn't planned to do so – hadn't planned, at that stage, anything at all. In her numbed state she had been acting – when capable of acting at all – entirely on impulse, and the impulse to speak the words "Christopher is dead" had been overwhelmingly strong.

Why so strong? What was it that had provoked so rash and unnecessary a revelation?

Partly, it was Bridget herself who had been the provocation; so self-assured, so well-informed, so jarringly rational in the midst of chaos. She was like a juggernaut, flattening in her path every non-rational consideration, utterly unaware of how they were all leaping back into life behind her as soon as she had passed . . .

And Bridget's voice, too. Norah remembered how that voice had gone on, and on, and on, sensible, rational, irrefutable, emphasising key syllables until they rang like hammer-blows through the big, quiet room . . . on and on and on, uninterrupted, as if she was delivering a lecture; as if this pleasant room with its easy-chairs was a lecture-hall, and Norah herself a whole class of students sitting on benches and hanging on the lecturer's words of wisdom.

Words of wisdom. Unquestioned rightness. This was what had provoked Norah, finally, into her ill-considered revelation. For the whole of Bridget's thesis, so carefully worked out, so clearly presented, so meticulously based on the data so far available – had been completely and ludicrously wrong. The one single bit of data known to Norah but not to Bridget made nonsense of it all, from the first sentence to the last, and the childish impulse to put Bridget in the wrong had been momentarily overwhelming: to put Bridget in the wrong, and at the same time to prove the innocence of her dead son.

All this she had achieved; and it was not until this morning, alone in the silent flat, that she began to realise the implications of what she had done.

Chapter 23

The short winter day was passing. The sky above the roofs opposite was no longer a dazzling midday blue, but hazed over with a silvery greyness; and still Norah sat on, staring through the big windows and in the grip of a curious inertia that was nothing to do with peace or relaxation. Rather, it was the paralysis of one awaiting some ordeal which cannot be averted but whose nature is still unclear.

Now and then, she tried to rouse herself from this unnatural lethargy, to pull herself together. More than once, she would find herself making a cup of coffee; and then, minutes later, there it would still be, nearly cold, and with skin forming on the surface.

It was unnerving. The passage of time seemed distorted in some way. Her initial sensation of relief at finding she had the flat to herself was dissolving, to be replaced by a panicky sensation of being in solitary confinement, cut off from all human aid.

What sort of aid? What actually was she afraid of? In the very process of asking herself the question, she already knew the answer perfectly well – had known it all along.

She was afraid of her husband; and she knew, now, exactly why she was afraid.

Crucial to Mervyn's own safety was that the body found on the Common should never be identified. The whole thing depended absolutely on no one but Mervyn knowing that Christopher was dead.

But one other person did know. Norah knew. Was it possible that by now Mervyn knew that she knew? Might Bridget have told him? Already? Or – almost as bad – might she, with her exaggerated sense of civic duty, have told the police?

Had she? Hadn't she? Did Mervyn know? Didn't he? With these questions going round and round in her head, unanswered, unanswerable, Norah drifted into a sort of uneasy sleep; and when she awoke, it was already dark. Her back, her shoulders, were stiff and aching, for she seemed to have slumped sideways against the wooden arm of the sofa when she fell asleep, and it had been sticking into her spine all this time. Edging herself painfully into a more comfortable position, she peered at her watch. Already she was hardly able to see the hands, but she just managed to make out that it was ten minutes to five.

Ten to five. Another two hours, before either of the others could be expected back, and in the meantime she was alone in the flat. The muzziness of her daytime sleep was receding, and memories of the past few hours came flooding back with a new and painful vividness. With the memories came the uneasy feeling that something had woken her. A slamming door? A noise in the street? At once Norah's nerves, temporarily dulled by sleep, were sharply on edge once more.

Had Mervyn tracked her down? *Could* he have done so? Certainly she herself hadn't given him the address – had indeed been at pains not to do so. The last thing she'd wanted in seeking this desperate place of refuge was any contact with her husband.

Could he, though, have discovered her whereabouts in some other way? Well, yes, he could. Might not Diana, in the course of that apparently successful interview with Christopher, have given the boy her address, or at least her phone number? ("So co-operative", she'd described him, and "So excited at the prospect of being on T.V.") What could be more likely than that she'd have encouraged this prospective interviewee by urging him to keep in touch? "Here's my card, do ring me if you have any questions", she might have said. Probably had said.

And Christopher would have left the card about, and Mervyn would have found it. Or, indeed, Christopher might actually have shown it to his father during one of his intermittentl, euphoric moods. "Look, I'm going to be on television!", he might have boasted brandishing the card: and Mervyn, whatever his thoughts at that moment might have been, would certainly have taken note of the address. And the telephone number.

By now, it was almost totally dark, but Norah somehow could not exert herself to switch on the lamp or to draw the curtains.

Could not exert herself to do so? Or was it that she did not dare to? Did not dare to reveal to the outside world that the flat was not empty after all? That someone was at home, and perhaps alone?

For Mervyn was after her – she was becoming more and more sure of it, and now her imagination leaped and swooped among the possibilities of what might happen next. *Anything* might happen – *anything*. Even while her mind was seeking a foothold in this featureless disaster area – at this very juncture, the telephone rang again.

Yes, again. The moment the sound began, she knew at once that this was the same sound that had roused her from sleep some minutes ago. For several seconds she simply could not move.

Of course, it might *not* be Mervyn. Indeed, it almost certainly wasn't. Both Bridget and Diana were constantly getting calls – not to mention Alistair, who was becoming such a fixture at this address.

But, on the other hand, it *might* be Mervyn; indeed, every single time the phone went, from now on, it *might* be him, and would therefore set her heart racing like this; would dry the saliva from her mouth, would make her knees shake and her stomach to contract with fear.

It stopped, of course, at last, but by this time she knew that if it went again she wouldn't be able to stand it. Not like this, all by herself, with the others all out. Before it went again, she must be out of the flat, out of the house, not to return until – by the lighted windows, the drawn curtains, and perhaps by the sound of the radio – she should know that her friends had returned, and she would no longer be alone.

Racing against time, against the temporarily quiescent phone whose next onslaught might come at any second, Norah snatched up her handbag, crammed on her coat and boots, and raced down the two long flights of stairs. As she neared the bottom she fancied she could hear the phone starting up again; but maybe she couldn't. Maybe it was in one of the other flats. Reaching the front door, and wrestling with the various burglar-proof gadgets which, in a multi-occupied building, one or other of the tenants always insists on, and always succeeds in obtaining, Norah finally wrenched the door open and burst into the cold and welcoming outdoors. She gasped with relief, and with the sudden rush of cold air into her lungs. She slammed the door shut behind her, and already felt her fear subsiding. Even if the telephone did go again, she wouldn't be able to hear it from here.

What next? There remained the best part of two hours to be filled in before either of her flatmates were likely to be back, and she couldn't just stand here on the steps for all that time. Norah looked up and down the road, seeking inspiration.

There were plenty of people about, scurrying purposefully this way and that. It was the rush hour, of course; they were all hurrying to get here or there by this time or that. She realized she must be just about the only one who was seeking to kill time rather than to beat it in the race to some destination.

Plenty of cars, too, several of them cruising along looking for somewhere to park. The houses here, once the dwellings of gentlefolk with large families and plenty of servants, were tall and spacious – almost grand, in a way – but virtually all of them had been sub-divided into flats, maisonettes and bed-sitters, the inhabitants of which, almost to a man, owned cars, and naturally enough, each sought to park his vehicle right outside his own front door. This meant, of course, an eternal tight-lipped competition for each four or five yards of frontage. Both Diana and Alistair complained constantly about this state of affairs, and were wont to argue, idly and inconclusively, about what *"They"* should do about it. Norah herself, not being a car-owner, never got involved in these discussions, though she'd noticed that Bridget – likewise a non-car-owner – would join in with gusto. Bridget was like that, which was one of the many reasons why Norah found her so intimidating.

For a minute or more, she stood still, half-way down the steps, gazing uncertainly this way and that. It was too early to expect either Diana's or Alistair's car to be joining the melée, but all the same Norah found herself half looking out for one or other of them – especially for Diana's buttercup-yellow Ford Escort, so easy to spot among the crowds This would be the direction Diana would be coming from, Norah mused, beginning to stroll, rather slowly, in the direction of the main road. She still hadn't decided where she was going, or how she was going to fill the next hour or so; but there was no doubt that she was beginning to feel better, out here in the cool air, and with familiar traffic noises all around. It was good, too, to be in the company of all these anonymous people from whom she had nothing to fear. They neither knew nor cared anything about her. They did not know that her son had just died, or that he'd been a schizophrenic, or anything at all.

It made her feel very safe.

"Well, well, my dear! Aren't you walking in the wrong direction?"

The voice came from behind her, and even before she had whirled round to face him, Norah could tell that her husband was smiling: that brilliant smile that he put on to reassure patients – or was it to intimidate them? In all these years she had never finally decided which.

It was a smile that revealed his fine set of teeth,

anyway, if that was any clue. She knew, too, what the teeth were going to look like under this sort of street lighting so white as to be almost greenish, and somehow more numerous than you would have expected in that narrow, tight-lipped mouth. Not that she had ever actually counted, of course: probably the patients hadn't either.

It couldn't have been more than a second before she turned round to face him, though it seemed much longer. And when she did, "Oh – Mervyn!" was all she could think of to say, while she waited for terror to engulf her.

For some reason, it hadn't so far. It was like stubbing your bare toe against a rock and waiting for the pain to reach your brain; often, it took a second or more. Ironic, too, that it had been to escape Mervyn that she'd rushed out of the flat into the safety of the street; and all the time it was in the street that he'd been waiting. Wasn't there something like this in the Bible? Someone fleeing to Samara to escape his appointment with Death in his home town, only to find that Death was right there in Samara, waiting for him?

"Come along," he was saying, taking her gently but firmly by the arm and steering her back in the direction from which she had come; "Come along, I want to talk to you" – and then, as she tried ineffectually to pull away from him, he went on: "What's the matter, my dear? What are you afraid of? It's *good* news I've got for you – very good news."

By now they had reached the front steps of Norah's current dwelling. He seemed to recognise it at once, and drew her to a standstill.

"Aren't you going to invite me in?" he inquired.

"There is a lot we have to talk about. About Christopher. I know how worried you've been about him lately, and I've come specially to reassure you about him. He's *all right*. He's more than all right, he's really getting to grips with his life and making sensible plans for the future. He's really happy, Norah. I had a letter this morning from the campsite he's staying at and he's having a great time. I'll show it to you when we get inside, you're going to be really pleased. He's not only having a good time now with his friends, but – Look, Norah, do let's get inside. How can I show you a letter out here in the dark? It's addressed to both of us, by the way; it starts off 'Dear Mum and Dad . . .'"

But Christopher is dead . . . She almost had to bite her tongue not to say the words aloud; and the very effort of keeping the words unspoken seemed to arouse in her a strange quiver of uncertainty.

Could she have been wrong? Could Mervyn possibly be telling the truth? Surely not. For one thing, the news he was purporting to convey was too good to be true. Far too good. Besides, the way he spoke had been just that little bit *too* soothing, *too* reassuring. This was the way a snake would speak to its hypnotised rabbit, if snakes could speak. Careful had been his whole speech, and well-rehearsed. The letter too, which he was planning to show her, it would be similarly careful, just like the last one. The small, cramped hand-writing would be almost like Christopher's, but not quite. The painstakingly concocted sentences would be just the sort of thing a boy of his age might write home to his parents . . . but they wouldn't be the sort of thing Christopher would write. Norah would recognise the

188

document as a forgery almost at once, of course she would.

But then what? Confront Mervyn then and there with her suspicions? Accuse him of bare-faced, calculated lying?

Never in the world would she be able to summon up that sort of courage. That sort of foolhardiness, rather – crazy, disastrous foolhardiness: because once Mervyn knew that she disbelieved his story, it wouldn't be long before he realised that she must at least suspect that their son was dead, and that Mervyn was responsible.

And then . . . and then? All alone in the flat, with no certainty as to when any of the others would come in . . .?

No, no. Soon she would be perusing the phoney letter, and as she did she must not allow the faintest quiver of doubt or suspicion to cross her face or to sound in her voice. "That's wonderful, Mervyn," she would have to say in response to whatever ludicrously rosy picture he'd concocted. Say it as if she meant it, too. Somehow contrive to make her tense features light up with the kind of delight that an anxious mother might be expected to feel at this sudden alleviation of her fears.

She couldn't do it. Just couldn't. While the agonisingly contrived smile might be held in place on her lips, what would be happening to her eyes? Eyes, the windows of the soul, through which all her grief, distrust and terror would be plainly seen, should Mervyn actually look into them while she was speaking. Of course, he often didn't look at her while she was speaking. Indeed, he mostly didn't. But on this occasion he would. Oh, how he would! Already she seemed to see those grey, shining eyes grow cold with hatred as

189

they gazed deep, deep into hers, plumbing her secret knowledge.

No, and no again. The only safe thing would be not to see the letter at all: to find some excuse for not inviting him into the flat and thus to evade him here and now, out in the safe, bustling street, surrounded by strangers, her unwitting protectors, under whose collective gaze he could not *force* her to invite him in.

Not force, no. But some things are stronger than force. What would he make of her lack of interest in this wonderful, reassuring letter from her son? How could a concerned and loving mother *not* want to see it? Her reluctance to do so would be as clear an indication of her disbelief as would any outright accusation of lying.

Besides, she *did* want to see it, didn't she?

Just in case.

In case of what? Nothing, of course; but all the same, in case. In case, in case . . .

"Well, all right," she found herself saying; and while she fumbled in her handbag for the keys, Mervyn sprang ahead of her up the steps so jauntily, and with such a mission-accomplished sort of air, that he might have been mounting a platform to receive some prestigious award: or, more realistically, as if gaining access to this building had been the sole object of his visit, and this object had now been triumphantly accomplished.

Chapter 24

"Nice place you've got here," Mervyn said pleasantly, like any well-brought-up visitor, as he looked around his wife's current living-room. And indeed the room was looking rather good this evening, with the standard-lamp throwing its warm light on the white walls and the heavy gold-brown curtains. It was tidy, too. This very morning, Bridget had scooped up for the paper-salvage all the outdated and unread newspapers and magazines that had littered the place for days. Diana's scatter-cushions, bright and variegated as a herbaceous border in high summer, looked their very best now that they no longer had to compete for house-room on the sofa with last week's Sunday supplements.

"Do sit down," said Norah, caught up willy-nilly in the hostess – visitor mode; and when her husband had settled himself under the lamp, she drew up a low stool embroidered in cross-stitch by Diana's grandmother, and tried to position herself so that the light would fall on Mervyn's features rather than her own; after which mini-precaution she ventured, with face slightly averted to take the forged letter from his outstretched hand.

And forged it was. She could see this without any doubt almost as soon as she had taken it from its envelope, and though this was exactly what she had been expecting all along, she was taken by surprise by the pang of pure disappointment that flashed through her. Until this moment, she had not realised that, somewhere deep in her heart, she'd been nursing a tiny spark of hope that maybe her husband wasn't lying; that maybe his fairy-tale happy ending for their troubled son was a reality; that Christopher was not only alive and well, but normal, magically cured of his mental illness.

Of course, it was not so. The very first sentence convinced her of that.

"Dear Mum and Dad,

You will be pleased to hear that we are now nicely settled under canvas, and are having a super time. The weather is glorious, and we're out all day walking in the hills . . ."

None of this was remotely like Christopher. He wouldn't have said any of these things, let alone written them. And had Mervyn really not noticed how long it was since their son had called them "Mum" or "Dad"? He had been addressing them as "Norah" and "Mervyn" for years now – how could his father be unaware of this? How could he possibly know so little about his own son?

The answer, of course, was simple when you thought about it. For years now, Mervyn had been deliberately setting himself *not* to know the truth about his son's mental condition: it was little wonder, then, that he'd ended up knowing almost nothing about the boy at all.

While Mervyn sat quietly under the lamp, never taking his eyes off his wife's face, she scanned the document as best she could. It was long – nearly five pages – and the forged script, cramped and tiny, was even harder to read than the genuine article would have been; but she persevered, and at last, with face still averted, she re-folded the document and replaced it in its envelope before handing it back to her husband. Already she had noticed the post-mark. The letter had indeed come from Derbyshire.

So he'd actually taken the trouble to drive up there to post it, in the interests of verisimilitude. What finesse, what determination!

Or was it sheer panic? And if so, to what further lengths might sheer panic take him?

"It sounds wonderful," she said carefully, exactly as she had planned to say it; "But . . ."

Here she stopped, appalled by her own indiscretion. She hadn't planned on any "Buts". She had intended to acquiesce in everything, to query nothing, to appear innocent of any doubts; and now here she was, on the verge of giving herself away. She had been just about to say: "But Mervyn, he can't possibly be going to do what he says here. How on earth can he go straight from a camping holiday in Derbyshire to a trek through North Africa without coming home first? What about clothes – passport – foreign currency?"

Almost, she had begun actually to worry about these things, before recalling that none of it was of the smallest importance because Christopher was dead.

Such a lot of things no longer needed to be worried about, now that Christopher was dead. Once again she was assailed by that strange sense of small darting lights in a great darkness; of a mighty weight having been lifted, leaving her relaxed and light, and curiously at peace. Even Mervyn himself seemed less of a burden, less to be feared, now that Christopher was dead.

Mervyn, too, was relaxing, she could feel it. For him, as well as for her, a moment of dreadful danger had been successfully bypassed. They were like two climbers, roped together, edging their way along some narrow and precarious ledge: the slightest loss of nerve, the slightest false step by either of them would have sent them both crashing onto the jagged rocks below.

No such false step had been taken, no such loss of nerve had been suffered, and so now here they were, in a place of comparative safety with the perilous abyss behind them: that is, with the forged letter safely unqueried between them.

No wonder it seemed like the time for a celebratory drink, even though the nature of the celebration was unmentionable; and when Norah expressed qualms about raiding her friends' drinks cupboard in their absence, what should be more natural than that Mervyn should reach into his brief-case for the bottle of whisky he had brought along.

"A present for you all," he explained, pouring a generous quantity into each of the glasses that Norah had set out on the small table. "I'd thought that your friends might be here too, actually: When are they coming back, do you know?"

Norah wasn't sure. Bridget, she guessed, would be in quite soon, she'd said something about having a lot of work to get through this evening in preparation for some event tomorrow. Diana, on the other hand, might be quite late, she was probably out with Alistair this evening.

Alistair? Who is Alistair? – and soon Norah found

herself giving her husband quite a detailed run-down on her flatmates and their various doings and avocations. He seemed really interested, asking her question after question, to which she responded as best she could. The whisky was beginning to go to her head; the narrow, restricted life which she had perforce endured during the last few years had virtually cut her off from normal social occasions, and her system had become unused to alcohol. She felt now as if her head was floating lightly on her shoulders, like a balloon. A pleasant enough sensation – very pleasant, in fact. It was pleasant, too, to find herself having a conversation with her husband which consisted of something other than defending herself against non-stop criticism. Indeed, far from criticising her present life style, or blaming her for having left him, he was showing himself quite unwontedly considerate and understanding.

"Well, Norah, dear, it does sound to me as if you've fallen on your feet for the time being. You seem to be pretty happy here, in this nice flat, and with these nice friends you've found. Why don't you stay on for a bit? I'm beginning to feel that you've maybe done the right thing – for us both. Perhaps a spell away from each other is just what we need. For a while, anyway."

Just what we need. Just what *you* need, anyway. So that I won't be there watching the post for letters that don't come from North Africa. So that when you tell me about that imaginary telephone call from Tripoli, I won't be able to say, But why didn't you call *me* to the telephone to speak to him?

That sort of thing. If I'm living somewhere else, it will be much, much easier for you to keep up the deception.

Easier, too, for me to pretend that I believe all these lies . . . But the sequence of her thoughts was becoming blurred now . . . difficult to follow. How much whisky *had* he given her? And was it neat? Had he forgotten to add water from the pretty cut-glass carafe that she'd brought in with the glasses? Or had he . . .? Was he . . .? She was trying, now, to respond to this suggestion of his that they should live apart for a while. She was trying to say "Yes", but somehow the word had become amazingly hard to pronounce: she tried and tried, but it just would not come.

I'm drunk, she thought wonderingly, and with a flicker of pride. I'm *really* drunk, for the first time in years! No, for the first time ever. I've never in my life felt as drunk as this, not even at those parties when I was young . . .

And this was the last thought she could clearly remember thinking.

Chapter 25

When, an hour or so later, Bridget arrived home and saw the male figure slumped in the armchair under the standard-lamp in the sitting-room, its long legs stretched out possessively across the pale carpet, she did not at once recognise it as Dr Payne. In fact, she thought for a moment that it was Alistair, and her relief at finding it wasn't was tempered only by her annoyance at finding who it was.

"There goes my quiet evening!" was her first thought – modified almost at once by the realisation that, unwelcome though he might be, the man wasn't *her* visitor. There was no reason why *she* should spend time entertaining him. He was Norah's.

Where *was* Norah, anyway?

"Where's Norah?" she asked, a trifle sharply, after the shortest possible exchange of greetings. "I suppose she knows you're here?"

For a few moments he did not answer, just looked her up and down in what seemed an unnecessarily intent scrutiny. Then:

"She's in her room," he said carefully. "Asleep, I have reason to suppose."

"*Asleep*?" The full bothersomeness of the situation burst upon her, and she was furious. She, Bridget,

197

was going to have to spend precious minutes doing something about this visitor, who wasn't hers at all. It was outrageous. Flat-sharing could only work if each member takes full responsibility for his/her own visitors, leaving the others free to get on with their lives. This was just about the most important of all the unwritten rules for this kind of sharing, and Norah had transgressed it unforgiveably.

Asleep, indeed!

"I'll go and wake her," she offered, as curtly as she dared, but was halted, as she turned towards the door, by the visitor's urgent protest.

"No, no! She's very tired. She's had a hard day, and I've persuaded her to go and lie down. And besides, Miss Sadler, it is not Norah whom I have come to see. It's yourself. It just happened that I ran into her outside, and she was kind enough to let me in so that I could wait for you indoors. As perhaps you've guessed, I have an important business matter to discuss with you. I have to have a word with you – in private . . ."

"With *me*? But you hardly know me. What *is* all this?" While she spoke, her curiosity by now aroused, Bridget was pulling up a chair so as to sit facing him across the coffee table. "What is it you want to say? I'm afraid I haven't a lot of time, and so . . ."

"Relax, my dear. It won't take a lot of time. The business we need to transact could take less than five minutes, so long as we are both sensible and rational about it. As I am sure we shall be. Already, from our admittedly short acquaintance, I have formed the opinion that you are an outstandingly sensible and rational young woman. Am I not right?"

"Look, Dr Payne, will you please get on and tell

198

me what you are driving at. As I've already told you, I haven't a lot of time. What is it you want to say to me? What have you come for?"

"Now, now Miss Sadler. Don't start playing silly games. Not with me. It doesn't suit you. You know perfectly well what I've come for. I want you to withdraw your allegations."

"My allegations?" For a moment Bridget was genuinely at a loss. Then: "Oh, you mean . . .?"

"Yes, that is precisely what I mean. Your allegations about a gun having been found in my garden. And about some fantastically unlikely behaviour on the part of my son Christopher. It has come to my ears that you have seen fit to take these bizarre inventions of yours to the police, and to report them formally as if they were facts. All I'm asking you to do is to withdraw these false statements. Now. Tonight."

"*Withdraw* them? I'm sorry, Dr Payne, but you must have taken leave of your senses. Of course I can't withdraw them. They are not 'false allegations', they are a true account of the facts, as you know perfectly well. We, the general public, were asked to report to the police any unusual incident we may have noticed around the time of the murder. These *were* unusual incidents, by anyone's standards, and so of course I reported them. It was my plain and obvious duty to do so. And, to be honest, Dr Payne, I can't understand why you should be so bothered about my revelations. You'd already handed in the gun found in your flower-bed, and so they must have realised already that . . ."

Her sentence stayed unfinished. That primitive and little-used instinct that warns of hidden danger coursed through her veins; and as she found herself staring into those heavy-lidded grey eyes, shining like polished metal in the lamplight, she became aware, also, of the unnatural stillness of those handsome, well-schooled features; and she knew, as clearly as if he had spoken the words aloud, that he *hadn't* handed in the gun to the police. Hadn't reported it, nothing. Her report, then, had been highly significant. It had been only this account of hers about the events of Sunday evening which had drawn police attention to Dr Payne's home at all. For the body still hadn't been identified. Perhaps it never would be. Christopher hadn't been reported missing. If it hadn't been for her conscientious visit to the police, there would have been nothing whatever to link the distinguished Dr Payne with the murder in any way. He knew this; and now she knew it too.

"All I'm asking you to do," he continued, in controlled and level tones, "Is to withdraw your statement. There will be no great difficulty about this, I assure you. It happens all the time, you know, in these sorts of cases. Some over-eager member of the public, yearning to see their picture in the papers, rushes off to the police with a cock-and-bull story which they hope will get them into the news. Or even on T.V.. And then, when they've cooled down, when they've gone home and thought about it, they get cold feet. They begin to realise that their story can't be substantiated, and that they may be getting themselves into all sorts of trouble. And so they scuttle back with their tails between their legs to withdraw it all. In my profession, I get called in to advise on this sort of thing quite often, and I'm familiar with the procedures. The worst that will happen to one of these impulsive romancers is a bit of a talking-to for wasting police time. However, since they've confessed and apologised – especially if they do so promptly, before any police time *has* been wasted, then the whole matter will be allowed to drop. And so this is why, my dear Miss Sadler, it's important that you should withdraw your allegations at once – this very night. For your own sake. I have my car here, I could give you a lift to the police station right now . . ."

"And if you did –" Bridget's voice was tight with fury "If you did, you do realise what I would say to them, don't you? I would report to them your intrusion into my home this evening, and I would inform them of your purpose in tracking me down. I would report to them word-for-word, everything you have been saying. I have been listening carefully, you know. Careful listening and accurate reporting back is part of my job . . ."

She sat back, waiting for the explosion of anger – fear – hatred – something. But it did not come. For several seconds he did not speak, but seemed to be studying her face, her whole demeanour, as if she was one of his patients: assessing her, no doubt, in accordance with some sort of psychological template.

Then, reaching into his breast-pocket, he pulled out a cheque book.

"Ten thousand pounds?" he suggested pleasantly. "As a young woman on your own, needing to earn every penny you get. I'd hazard a guess that . . ."

"Dr Payne, will you please leave this house? Immediately! Or would you like me to call the police?"

"Now, now, my dear – not so hasty! Though I do admire your spirit, I really do!" Here he paused, studying her face yet again, assessing his chances. Every man has his price, you could see him thinking: and every woman, too. It was several seconds before he spoke.

"How about twenty thousand . . .?"

Bridget started up from her chair, intent on phoning the police as she had threatened. She couldn't really afford so much as a moment's delay – but the temptation was too great. Leaning across the low table, she slapped his face as hard as she possibly could. She was a sturdy girl, and those strong muscles were rendered even more effective at this moment by the rush of adrenalin which was flooding her whole body.

It was wonderful! She stood back, gazing with the satisfaction of an inspired artist at her completed handiwork: one side of his face blazing scarlet with the force of her blow; the other side white as paper with alarm and dismay.

But by this time her chance to reach the telephone was over. His muscles, too, were powered by a flood of adrenalin; he had her arm in an iron grip, forcing her back onto her chair.

"So you want to play it rough, do you, dear?" he enquired, controlling his voice with audible effort. "Very well, then that's how we'll play it"; and plunging his free hand into his briefcase, he brought out a hand-gun. The very same one, as far as Bridget could tell, that they had found in his front garden.

"I'm sorry it has had to come to this," he said. "I really am. I had hoped we could come to some mutually satisfactory arrangement, but since your obstinacy has rendered this impossible, I have no alternative but to resort to more forceful methods to bring you to your senses."

Raising the gun, he pointed it – perhaps merely as a threat – in her direction.

"Well, my dear, does this encourage you to change your mind?"

He had released his grip on her arm by now, but she still sat quietly in the chair into which she had been pushed. It seemed sensible in the circumstances, with that gun only the width of a coffee-table away. Indeed, it *was* sensible. The mistake she made, though, was to laugh.

"You must be out of your mind," she taunted him, "If you think you can scare me with that silly implement. It's as obvious to me as it must be to you that you aren't planning to lumber yourself with a second murder charge. You're going to have trouble enough disentangling yourself from the first one, without courting another one from which there will be no chance whatever of escape. I mean, it will be an open and shut case, won't it?

"For a start, Norah can vouch for the fact that you arrived here this evening, and I daresay other people in the house will have noticed you coming in – not to mention passers-by in the street – neighbours and so forth. And so when I'm found shot through the head in my own sitting-room, and when everyone else in the house will have heard the shot, and will have heard the shot, and will be lined up in their doorways all agog to know what's happening, while you make your getaway past all those doors, down those flights of stairs . . . Well, it's ludicrous, isn't it? What sort of a fool do you think I am, to believe that you'd ever let yourself in for that sort of scenario . . .?"

"How right you are, my dear! *What* a clever girl! But you see, dear, it won't *be* like that. You forget, you see, that I'm a psychiatrist of some note, and I can explain to them that you are my patient. I shall tell them that I have been treating you for some time for depression.

Normally, of course, you come to my consulting rooms for your sessions, but on this particular occasion you rang me up in very great distress, begging me to come to you in your own home, and threatening suicide if I should fail to arrive. In my position, and with my current knowledge of your case, I could not do other than take the threat seriously, and make all speed to your address. Once there, I will be able to tell them, I found you distraught and hysterical, and repeating your threats of suicide. You were in a frantic state of guilt about some grotesquely false story you'd told to the police yesterday. Guilt, you know, is an almost invariable concomitant of depression, and the patient commonly feels herself driven to suicide as a way of punishing herself for the guilty deed.

"All this is perfectly plausible, indeed commonplace, as my colleagues will readily confirm. The tragic outcome in this case is that my patient, unknown to me, had somehow equipped herself with a loaded hand-gun; and even while I was talking to her, endeavouring to alleviate her sense of guilt at having deceived the police, she snatched it up and shot herself before I could make a single move to prevent her.

"Tragic; and of course your neighbours will have heard the shot. Of course they will come out to see what has happened, and no doubt they will give me every assistance in coping with this tragic event . . . telephoning the doctor, the police. Giving me cups of hot sweet tea for my state of shock. . . .

"They won't believe it!" Bridget retorted sturdily, trying to sound more confident that she felt. "Of course they won't. They know me. They know I'm not *like* that!"

"You may be a very clever girl Miss Sadler. In fact I'm sure you are, as I've just told you. But you are also somewhat naïve. Have you not heard, or perhaps read in some popular magazine article, that depressives tend to be deeply ashamed of their condition? They will go to great lengths to hide it from their friend and workmates, putting on a false front of extreme self-confidence and cheerfulness, when inside they are a seething mass of despair? This is a well-known syndrome; and it is especially prevalent among successful career women. Women, perhaps, who are approaching their thirties, still with no male partner: women who are beginning to wonder what is the point of it all? Where is their success getting them? Is it bringing them love? Happiness? Contentment?

"The answer, all to often, is, no, it is not; and the woman is then in a fearful dilemma. She has to pretend, all the time, among friends, colleagues – everybody – to be still the person she once was – brilliant, indefatigable, on top of the world; while all the time her energy is draining away – she is no longer in her first youth . . . Though of course, Miss Sadler, I am not implying that *you* are no longer in your first youth . . ."

"Of course you're implying it! What would be the point of all this psycho-babble if that wasn't the implication? But you're forgetting one thing, Dr Payne. If I've been your patient for a sufficient number of weeks, for this sort of story to be plausible, then my records would be in the hospital files. Or are you planning to cook the hospital records? Not so easy these days, when they're all on computer . . ."

"Oh dear, that clever little brain of yours thinks of everything doesn't it? But once again you are wrong. You're one of my *private* patients, you see, and the records are entirely in my hands. I do have private patients, you know, as well as my hospital appointments A lot of us do. . . ."

He paused, fingered the gun almost lovingly with his gloved hand, then looked up again.

"Another thing, my dear, that may not have occurred to you: your finger-prints are all over this gun already. Suicide will *have* to be the verdict."

Bridget caught her breath – inaudibly, she hoped. So that was why the gun was at the bottom of a plastic bag, so that whoever took it out would leave it covered with fingerprints other than those of Dr Payne. It didn't matter whose they were – anyone's would be enough to put the authorities off the true scent.

The whole scenario now seemed clear. The original plan had doubtless been that a gang of imaginary burglars should have broken into the house and have shot Christopher dead when he caught them in the act. No doubt the house was to appear ransacked, it was all to have happened on that very Sunday afternoon; but the timing had gone disastrously wrong. Christopher was out somewhere, leaving no clue as to when he could be expected back, and on top of this the three tiresome females had come barging in and stayed for hours, creating further havoc with the remaining options. A new, last-minute plan had to be concocted, and quickly. No wonder it had been full of loose ends.

With Bridget out of the way, though, Mervyn might yet get away with it. She was the one who had kept her head, had reported what she knew to the police. Above all, she was the only person, so far as he knew, who had guessed that Christopher was dead. She was the one who would have no compunction about reporting

206

to the police anything else that she happened to find out – including the whole of this evening's interview: the attempted bribery: the threats.

Across the table, Dr Payne was still fiddling, idly, thoughtfully, with the gun.

"I hate doing this," he said. "I really do. Are you *sure* you wouldn't rather have twenty thousand pounds? You could go on a world cruise. You could buy a yacht. You could start a new life . . ."

He raised the gun, purposefully, and leaned towards her, taking aim.

"I'm sorry to bring it so close to you," he apologised, "But I don't want to miss, and cause you unnecessary pain."

He paused, seemed to hesitate.

"Are you sure?" he repeated, "Are you quite, quite sure that you wouldn't rather have twenty thousand pounds?"

I *won't* be scared, Bridget told herself. I *won't*. Once you've let your self get scared, you've already let your enemy win. I won't. I won't, I won't!

Once more, for the second time that evening, she made her disastrous mistake.

She laughed.

"I don't believe it's even loaded!" she jeered, reaching for it across the table.

The noise was like the end of the world; but, strangely, she felt no pain. It was as if a mighty hand had lifted her from her chair and laid her, quite gently, full-length on the floor.

I hope I'm not bleeding onto our lovely carpet, was her last thought before losing consciousness.

But she was; she was.

Chapter 26

It was during her second day in hospital after the operation to remove the bullet from her rib-cage that Bridget was allowed to receive vistors, and reluctantly, propped against pillows, she prepared to do so.

For really and truly, given the choice, she would have preferred not to have any visitors at all. The invalid role was anathema to her. Absolutely not her thing. She was the strong one, the always-well one; the one who could boast of never having had a day's sick-leave in all her working life. It was *other people*, weaker and more fragile human specimens than herself, who found themselves in hospitals, in doctor's surgeries, on sick-leave: humbled recipients of largesse in the form of flowers and grapes and get-well cards. These were the people, quite unlike herself, who needed to be asked how they were feeling, and to be listened to as they answered.

Bridget wished for none of this. Given the choice, she would have chosen to be left entirely on her own – reading, listening to the radio, working as best she could, until she was on her feet again completely recovered.

But of course she wasn't being given the choice. No one is. Once in hospital, you are a sitting-duck for anyone who chooses to come to your bedside: you

209

have no control over who they are, when they come, or how long they stay. At home, you can, as a last resort, pretend to have an appointment with somebody else, but here there could be no such escape route.

She would have to go through with it. She would have to respond to the sympathy, to the kind enquiries. She would have to explain, to one after another of them that, yes thank you, she was feeling fine, and that the surgeon had promised complete recovery in days rather than weeks; back at work, probably, inside a month. It could have been so much worse. The bullet had mercifully missed both her heart and her lungs, though it had been a near thing. It could have been much, much worse.

Well, yes, of course it could have been worse. She might have been having to tell her visitors that she wasn't feeling fine at all, but absolutely awful, and that the surgeon had warned her that it would be a long business and might leave her unable to continue with her chosen career. Of course that would have been worse. Of course she was lucky that it was only this; but all the same it was humiliating to be ill at all. Even more humiliating to have been saved by Alistair, who had let himself into the flat before Mervyn had had time to fire a second shot.

Bracing herself for she knew not whom, and resolving to behave nicely to whoever it was, she felt quite a little rush of relief when she saw that her first visitor was to be Diana, tap-tapping across the ward, her face alight with happiness, and her bright hair swinging as she moved.

She was pleased, of course, to find Bridget so much better and out of danger, but to Bridget's enormous relief she did not spend many words on solicitous enquiries, but plunged straight ahead into an account of the real source of her radiant looks.

"It's been confirmed!" she exulted. "There's absolutely no doubt at all any more! I *am* pregnant! July it will be . . . Isn't that marvellous!"

One couldn't agree, in all honesty, that it *was* marvellous; to Bridget it all seemed most ill-judged. But she was surprised to find herself feeling much more benign towards the project than she had before. Was it sheer physical weakness that was softening her capacity for clear and practical judgement? – the anaesthetic, perhaps, or the loss of blood? Or was she genuinely seeing the thing in a new way? After all, you only live once, and if in this one and only life of yours there is something you want as passionately as Diana wanted this baby, and if it is something that brings you as much joy as was now shining in her friend's face – should you not grab it with both hands and be thankful? And who could tell that Diana wouldn't make a success of being a single mother? Lots of women did. More and more of them with every passing year. Likewise, with every passing year, the child of a one-parent family must be feeling less and less exceptional. Indeed, by the time this one was of school-age, one-parent families could well have become the norm.

"Mummy, why have I only got one Daddy?" an anxious five-year-old could be asking after his first week at school.

"But it won't *be* a one-parent family!" cried Diana, as Bridget began to expound something of her new philosophy. "You won't believe this, but Alistair is actually *pleased*! Yes, I know I said I wasn't going to tell him just yet, but . . . well, it sort of came out.

211

And he was *pleased*! Didn't I tell you he would be? He even went out and bought a copy of the Dictionary of Christian Names, and he's been hunting out the most ghastly names you can possibly imagine. 'Genghis Khan,' 'Assurbanipal,' that sort of thing. Well, you know how he is. He wouldn't bother to do that sort of thing if he wasn't thrilled to bits, would he? Besides, I feel sure it's going to be a girl . . ."

She chattered on and Bridget, listening to her, found it impossible not to feel, however irrationally, that such happiness as this was going to be worth whatever it cost.

And who knew? Alistair might, after all, turn out to be a devoted father. Goodness knows, he was inconsistent enough; there was just no telling.

"He's coming to see you later on," Diana was saying as she gathered up her belongings and prepared to leave. "I expect he'll tell you all about it – if not, you must ask him. Because he really *is* pleased, you know, and I'd like you to hear for yourself what he says."

What Alistair said turned out to be not quite what Bridget had been led to expect.

"I shall marry her, of course," he announced, helping himself to a substantial cluster of Bridget's grapes. "Well, it's what a chap is supposed to do, isn't it, in this situation? But don't worry. The more I think about it, the more I don't see why it should make any difference to any of us. We can all go on living comfortably exactly as we are now, with me dropping in and out when I feel like it, just as I do now. I'll be keeping on my own place, of course. Nothing odd about that, not these days. All the best people are doing it. All the most trendy and newsworthy couples – especially the super-high-brow ones – are opting for this life-style; and making a go of it, too, by all accounts. 'Go' being the operative word, of course. Staying becomes much more acceptable once you have the option of going.

"No, Bridget, don't be silly; *of course* you'll stay on at the flat. Like I say, we can all carry on exactly as we do now. I'll be married to Diana, that's true, but I can still go on yearning after you, can't I? And don't look like that, you know perfectly well that I've been yearning after you all this time. I like your spiky ways, and married men really do need someone to yearn after as well as a wife. There are good historical precedents for that, too. Look at Shelley, yearning after Mary's half-sister. And Dickens, too; wasn't there a yearn-worthy sister-in-law in his household? Though of course it depends on which biography you've been reading; but such a well-read know-all as you, Bridget . . ."

Bridget could have kicked herself for her strange inability to think quickly enough of an appropriately devastating put-down. Normally, her quick tongue would have been ready enough with some abrasive retort; but not now. Some sort of power seemed to have drained out of her; and after Alistair's departure she was appalled to find tears trickling weakly down her face; tears partly of weakness, and partly of an idiotic kind of pleasure. She was actually feeling *flattered* by the man's silly remarks. What on earth had happened to that strong, sensible self which was the only self she knew?

It would return, of course, as soon as the effects of the anaesthetic and the shock had worn off, but meantime she was undergoing some strange reversals of feeling. When, later that same evening, her mother arrived, tearful with relief at finding her daughter on the way to recovery, Bridget found herself weeping too, uncontrollably; tears of relief, and love, and long-ago childlike dependence, in her mother's arms.

It wouldn't last, of course. By the very next morning she could already feel, in her fast-healing body, the beginnings of returning strength and vigour, and this, of course, she found immensely reassuring.

Reassuring, yes, but something in her had changed, and would stay changed. She would be strong again, and brave again, but never again would she be a person who did not know what it was like to be weak. It was a piece of knowledge to be added to her already extensive store, and it would never be forgotten.

Chapter 27

The following afternoon, Bridget received a surprise visitor. A young woman was hurrying lightly, purposefully across the ward, and for a moment Bridget couldn't put a name to her. The face was familiar, certainly – but who . . .? where . . .? It was a face she'd seen quite recently – and now, in a flash, she remembered *where* she'd seen it. On a mantelpiece. The mantelpiece over the fireplace in Norah's home.

Yes, it *was* Norah; it really was – but what a transformation! For a moment, Bridget fancied that the unhappy lady must suddenly have bought herself a lot of new, smart clothes . . . must have had her hair done in a new style – something like that. But no, at a second glance, Bridget realised that her hair was still the same tight, gingery-grey frizz. She wore the usual cardigan, the usual nondescript blouse. What was different was her face, her walk, her whole demeanour. Even her *height* was altered, now that her cringing stance had been replaced by straight, swinging shoulders and a lifted head.

What could have caused so startling a transformation, at a time of such unmitigated disaster in the poor woman's life? Her son was dead; her husband on a murder charge. What on earth could have caused such rejuvenation?

The disaster itself, of course. However much a disaster sweeps away, it also inevitably leaves a slate clean, and its born-again victim has nowhere to go but forward. Around her, even before she knows it, doors have been flung open by the very force of the storm. Newness shines in her face long, long before it penetrates her mind.

Of course, Norah had first to ask Bridget how she was, and of course Bridget had to answer; but almost at once they found themselves piecing together, on the basis of what each already knew, the probable sequence of events on that fatal Sunday afternoon. There seemed little doubt that a phoney break-in was what Mervyn had first tried to organise. Christopher was to be found dead indoors, with a bullet through his head; and the gun that the imaginary robbers had used would be found discarded in the garden. A son who had died heroically fighting off burglars would be a far, far more creditable son to boast of than the ever-deteriorating mental wreck which was the alternative.

But the plan had misfired. Christopher had wandered off somewhere: he had not returned home at the appropriate time to play his appointed part in this scenario, and Mervyn had panicked. Those same agonising questions that Norah had so often had to ask herself were now homing in on Mervyn. Where *is* he? What is he up to? Who is he upsetting? What sort of disgrace is he bringing the family into *this* time? For the first time, it was the father, not the mother who had to face these questions. For the first time he had to cope, to decide by himself what to do. He was aware, by this time, that Christopher was mad, and that his madness was escalating with terrifying speed into one of his worst

216

manic phases. Possibly – indeed, probably – he had been talking to his father in exactly the way he had talked to Bridget. "You are my creature," he would have said: "I genetically engineered you . . . You can only do what I've programmed you to do."

The child is father of the man: a new and horrifying gloss on the old proverb.

For Mervyn, compelled at last to awake from his years of self-imposed blindness, it had been too much. Too terrifying. Too humiliating. To have *this* son roaming the neighbourhood in *this* sort of state . . . He had *got* to be found, and urgently. After the three intrusive women had at last left, and when Christopher still hadn't got home, Mervyn had gone, gun in hand, in search of him.

Had he guessed the boy would be wandering on the Common, intent on some crazy project? Or had he tracked him down elsewhere, and lured him into the car for his last, fatal journey? Whichever it was, the deserted Common, after dark, must have seemed like a good place, with its dark bushes and overhanging dripping trees.

"I could blow up the world!" Christopher had boasted to Bridget on that Sunday afternoon. Was this what he believed he had done, as the noise roared through him, just as it had roared through Bridget? Had it been as painless for him as it had been for her? Did he die in triumph, world destroyer, world creator, King of the World?

While they talked, sometimes even laughing at some bizarre little incident that one or other of them recalled, speculations about Mervyn escalated. Right now, probably, the story was being pieced together by the police.

He had no defence, of course, having been caught red-handed.

Somehow, Norah couldn't bring herself to care, one way or the other. It all seemed too complicated to care about. It was beyond the range of her still-battered emotions.

They both laughed a little, guiltily, uneasily. Norah was still feeling vaguely surprised to find herself laughing, even at a time like this. A time like what? She had not yet in any way faced the vastness of her freedom, the multiplicity of the options that would soon be edging their way into her field of vision.

The process would begin very gradually, of course. Indeed, in a very small way, it had begun already. Only that morning, she'd picked up the telephone and had heard the voice of her neighbour and confidante, Louise. The voice, as of old, was once again bubbling over with warm and eager curiosity. Once again it was the voice of friendship; a cup of tea was being offered, and the prospect of a long, long talk.

"Why don't you pop in?" Louise had said, and Norah, for the first time in years, and without any qualms or backward glances at what might be going on at home, was able to say "Yes, I'd love to."